Rose's Triumphant Return

Phyllis A. Collmann

Library of Congress Control Number: 2003092606

ISBN: 1-57579-262-1

Cover painting by Jeannie Nemmers.

Printed in the United States of America
Pine Hill Press
4000 West 57th Street
Sioux Falls, S.D. 57106

 *Dedication*

To my husband Colin
for 51 years of marriage and
for his devoted love and support.

To my children,
Cynthia, Kimberly, Ronald and Melonie.

I love you.

A Special Thank You

Julie Ann Madden
Diane Den Napel
Jeannie Nemmers

About the Author

Phyllis A. Collmann is a retired nurse. She lives on a farm with her husband of 51 years. This is her third book. It is a sequel to her first book called, "Rose's Betrayal and Survival" Phyllis enjoys writing pioneer stories. This book continues the exciting life of Rose Donlin.

Published Books:
Rose's Betrayal and Survival
Kim's Unplanned Saga
Rose's Triumphant Return

Rose's Triumphant Return

PHYLLIS A. COLLMANN continues her story about Rose Donlin.

The date is 1885. Rose's life was about to change again. The new journey would again take her from St. Louis to Oklahoma City. Her abduction from the train was painful and horrendous for her.

Escaping from her kidnapper meant stealing his horse and riding horseback for nearly one month. He stalked her all the way.

The exciting adventures for her includes a young man named Henry, who rides with her and protects her.

Join Rose on a trip across the wilderness fighting the elements of rain, snow, crossing rivers, hostile men and indians. Going without food, sleeping on the cold ground, and much more.

Chapter 1

Rose Donlin was about to go on another journey she would never forget. She was 22 years old, and at times she felt she had lived forever. The year was 1885.

Rose knew it would be very difficult to take her father back to Oklahoma City. He had so many excuses not to go. First he had no money, then what would he do with his home.

After she had finished eating breakfast with her father, Rose went back to her room. Everything in her room reminded her of her mother. The curtains, rugs and the rag dolls looked the same as the day she had been forced to leave it five years ago.

Rose had visioned her room nearly every day while she lived in the cabin with Joseph Higgins. At first it was an angry vision because it had been her father's decision to send her to Oklahoma. As the time passed, the vision of her room in her mind just became a picture, because she had accepted her room in Joseph's cabin.

When Rose's mother first became ill, she had insisted they have a picture taken of her precious family. The picture had been with Rose for the five years she had been gone.

When Rose arrived at Joseph's cabin she could not bear to look at the picture, for every time she did, she would cry until her eyes would nearly swell shut. She reached in her satchel and gazed at the faces in the frame. Her father was right; she looked exactly as her mother did in the picture when Rose was 12 years old. Her father looked so young. He had no gray hair like he had now.

Louis Donlin had agreed to go back to Oklahoma with Rose, only after Rose pleaded with him to see an eye doctor in Oklahoma. Louis had to close up his homestead, and ask his neighbor to check on it while he was gone. His plan was that he would only be gone away a short period of time.

Rose needed to reminisce, one last time. She left her father's home and walked toward the Missouri River. She had spent most of her young life swimming or helping with her father's traps. She remembered doing the same thing five years ago as she was doing now, after she had finished packing all of her books in the wooden box her father had brought home from the general store.

Rose sat down along the bank in the sun. A few feet away was her father's canoe. She had been allowed to take it out on the water whenever she had wanted. It was much larger then Joseph's. Her father always told her the river could be dangerous, even when it's calm.

∽ Chapter 2 ∽

The sun shinning on the water made it glisten. The warmth off the water made her feel relaxed and calm. Rose laid back on the bank near the water. She closed her eyes and drifted off in a restless dream. The image she saw was the face of the man that had attacked her when she crawled out of the water in her private inlet, while in Oklahoma.

His eyes were large and staring at her. Rose could feel his hands on her body. She woke with the fear it was real and happening now. Jumping to her feet, she realized she was alone. Why was she so frightened of this man?

Rose left the river, trying to erase the man's face from her mind.

As she reached her childhood home, she hoped someday she could bring her own family to see where she had grown up.

The horse and buggy were tied to her father's gate. She entered the house and picked up her satchel and took one last look around her father's home. Rose helped her father lock up the house, and then helped him step up into the buggy. She directed the horse toward the livery stable.

Chapter 3

The train station was only a short distant to walk from the livery stable. Rose took hold of her father's arm and steered him along.

The clothes Rose wore were of the latest fashion from Oklahoma City. People turned and looked at her as she and her father walked on the board sidewalk. Rose was a very beautiful young woman. A man was walking toward them, and Rose only got a glimpse of him as he swiftly walked past. A little shiver ran up her spine.

Rose carried her satchel, and in it were the most important possessions she had. The picture of her family, the paper John had given her, proving how wealthy she had become since Joseph had died. The cash she carried was a large amount. The log she had written in for the five years while she lived with Joseph in his cabin in Oklahoma. The written material was the size of a book, for she had left nothing out.

The obligation Rose felt to Joseph was extremely important to her. She was adamant on letting everyone in Oklahoma know what an honorable man Joseph Higgins was.

Rose told her father when to step up as they entered the train station, then she instructed him to sit down on the waiting bench. She purchased two tickets for the two-day trip to Oklahoma City.

The train was on time so they had only a short wait. They stood on the platform as the train pulled up, and the conductor yelled out, "All aboard." Then gave the destination of the train.

Boarding the train took only a few minutes; everyone seemed to want to help a beautiful young woman with an older man who could not see.

The train began to move in little jerks. The grinding of the steel train wheels on the steel tracks made a loud, shrieking, clanging noise. The black smoke from the burning coal billowed up into the air. Everyone sat silent until the train was moving.

Rose explained to her father what direction they were facing, and how many seats were in their section of the train. The seats were all filled with families with little children, elderly couples, and older women traveling alone. She told him all she could to make him comfortable for the two day trip ahead of them.

They ate a small amount from the sack lunch Rose had packed, and her father leaned his head back and closed his eyes. His breathing changed and she knew he was asleep.

She reached into her satchel and carefully pulled out her log. It was as if she was living the first day all over again. It was the summer after her 17th birthday. She had been to the river for a swim while her father took his furs into St. Louis, Missouri. When he returned the next day, nothing in her life was ever the same.

Her story began, September 25, 1880. My father returned with a telegram saying I was going to go to Oklahoma City, where I was to marry a man I did not know and spend the rest of my life with him. The ride on the train was so rough, at times the train jolted, feeling as if it would tip off of the tracks. I could smell smoke when the wind blew it toward my car. Nothing in my young life could have prepared me for the next five years. I read books and tried not to think of how alone I felt. No one paid any attention, or looked at a poorly dressed girl, traveling alone. I left the first train and entered the train that would take me the rest of the way. A nicely dressed man met me when the train arrived in Oklahoma City. I was hoping he was the man I was sent to marry. He was not. He introduced himself as John Fitzpatrick, friend of Joseph Higgins. His buggy was waiting to take me to Joseph's.

⌒◡ Chapter 4 ◡⌒

Suddenly Rose was aware of the train beginning to slow down. She stopped reading and laid her papers back in her satchel. Her father opened his eyes and moved in his seat. Rose could feel his body tense up. The train came to a complete grinding stop.

The train stopped so unexpectedly many passengers nearly fell, and some children fell from their seats screaming.

Her father spoke, and each word was filled with more fear. He said, "Rose, please tell me what's happening." Louis could hear the whispering, and the horses and riders yelling as they rode along side the train. His biggest concern was how could he help Rose when he was unable to help himself.

Rose looked out the window, and they were stopped in a desolate area. She could see hills off in the distance. Then she saw men on horses riding along the train with handkerchiefs over their faces.

Everyone on the train started to talk loudly and then jumped up and looked out of the windows at the dark skinned, dark hair, scruffy looking men on horseback.

Rose could hear the men hollering in loud voices. The language was Spanish. She had heard it spoken at the general store when she went with her father to trade his furs. Her father had always warned her not to listen or get close to anyone of the men. Her father also told her they were always on the move, looking for an easier life by taking from the rich or poor.

A man dressed in a railroad workman's uniform, opened the door and tried to calm the frightened passengers. He told everyone to get back in their seats and not to fight.

He said, "These men will kill anyone who does not do what they say or give them all of their possessions. Just give them what you have and they will leave. We hope no one gets hurt."

"Rose," her father's voice was whispering, "Please, just give them what they want."

Rose did not answer her father; she reached over and patted his arm to reassure him. She did not intend to give one thing of her valuable property to a man who steals. She leaned down and opened her satchel. The revolver was lying on the bottom. Joseph had told her, "Always keep it loaded, but hidden from view." Her hand pulled it out close to her body and slipped it under her dress and into her camisole. The other articles she took out were a pair of bloomers and a slip. She opened her father's box that held his belongings, and laid them on top.

Rose could hear the shouting from the other train cars getting closer. She could hear wives saying to their husbands, "Give them what they want; please don't make them shoot you." Children were crying while mothers tried to get them to be quiet.

Rose leaned very close to her father's ear and said, "I'll be back, do not move."

"No, Rose, no," he said, in a desperate low tone. Rose answered, telling him she would be right by his side when the robbers got to their car.

Rose reached down for her satchel, putting it under her coat. She hurried to the next train car where the ladies closet was located. She entered the tiny space. Her eyes searched for a hiding place. The room had one drawer, pulling it open, she took out all the feed sack towels. Rose stuffed her satchel in, and packed the towels over and around it. She pulled on the cord from the ceiling in case someone had seen her go in. The water flushed the commode.

Moving swiftly through the car to again take her seat next to her father. She touched his arm.

"Rose, I only have a small amount of money." Her father's voice sounded almost tearful. "Father," Rose answered saying, "Give it all to them."

Rose began again by saying, "Father, if something happens and we get separated, when you get to Oklahoma City, tell John Fitzpatrick what has happened. Also tell him to go to the ladies' closet on this train and look in the hand wipe drawer."

The door flung open, the noise was loud and frightening. The children clung to their mothers. You could hear muffled cries, mothers putting their hand over their children's mouth; so they would not anger the men more.

Rose reached over and held her father's hand. The bandit's boots pounded on the wooden floor as they darted back and forth behind Rose and her father, grabbing money and jewelry from each adult passenger. The men's voices were getting louder as they made their way up the aisle toward Rose and her father.

Rose could hear three different men. She listened and counted. She knew if she showed her gun, they would shoot her. She also feared for her father's life.

She sat waiting for them to get to her. The hand on her shoulder was almost painful.

"You're next lady, I want everything you have." The voice's accent was sharp and distinct. Rose looked up into large dark eyes. He was wearing a bandana over his face. For a few seconds, they stared at each other.

This couldn't be. But his eyes were the same, something penetrated into her mind and she couldn't move.

He roughly stuck out his hand and motioned for her to give up her money. Her father laid his few dollars in his hand. This angry man was not going to give up. He had seen her holding her father's hand.

He leaned down close to her face and said, "If you don't give me your money, I'm going to take this old man with me." Instantly Rose was ready to fight, and defend her father.

"No, no," she yelled back at him.

"Where's your bag?" He asked impatiently.

"My clothes are in his box," She told him. The man tore open her father's cardboard box, on top was Rose's underwear. He kicked the box with his boot, sending it back under their seat.

⟶ Chapter 5 ⟵

He reached out and firmly took hold of both of her arms, pulling Rose to her feet. Her father stood up beside her, yelling, "Leave her alone, you no good bastard."

Rose jerked toward her father, and said, "Listen, I'm alright. You remember and do exactly what I told you."

Rose was being roughly pulled back down the aisle, with the man's hand firmly holding her arm. He opened the door so hard it slammed against the wall. They stepped through, and they were at the outside steps leading off of the train.

He took the three steps down and turned back to her. He let go of her arm, then swiftly put both of his hands around her tiny waist and lifted her to the ground. She wanted to fight back but she was afraid some other scoundrel would see her, panic would set in and they would kill her.

Men were riding up and down on both sides of the train screaming and yelling. The angry man waived his arm and screamed at a rider. The rider rode toward a horse tied to the side of the train. He rode up by Rose leading the horse and handed the reins to the man who appeared to be their leader.

Without any warning, Rose felt herself being lifted up and over the horse. She had no choice, but to throw her legs over the saddle. Her dress was circled fully around the saddle. He reached for the saddle horn while jumping on the back of the horse. She had no time to react.

Rose felt his leg move hard into the horse's lower part of the stomach. The horse surged forward. It was in a full gallop in seconds. He had pulled on the reins, and they were heading away from the train. One of his hands held both reins, the other hand was tightly around Rose. Her hope now was that he could not feel the gun.

Rose's beautiful black hat was left behind on the seat of the train beside her father. Her hair hung nearly to her waist, and the wind was blowing it straight back into the angry man's face. At first he didn't say anything, then when he couldn't see at all, he told her to tie it back, or he was going to cut it off with his knife.

By the sound of his voice, she knew he would do it. She pulled her hair down and put it under her dress collar.

Chapter 6

They rode for what seemed for hours. She tried to lean forward, and he kept pulling her to him.

The land was changing. The flat ground was behind them, and they were entering the bluffs and tree area. The horse was not running as fast. They were going up hill and it was tiring him.

Rose yelled out, "Your horse needs water."

"We only have a few more miles, and I know where the watering hole is." He yelled back at her. "I only hope its not dried up." He added.

He continued to push his horse, which was frothing at its mouth. Rose's body was full of pain; every muscle ached. The ride had jostled her for what seemed an awful long time. The man showed no mercy for Rose or his horse.

Rose felt the horse slow as the dark- skinned man tugged back on the reins. She looked around, wondering why here? Then she saw the small watering hole. The outside edge was dry, with chips of dirt curling up. A small amount of water remained. He rode the horse right up to the water. He slid off while dropping the right rein and holding onto the left.

He then reached back up and lifted her down. He lifted her high up over the horse, turned her to him, and then slowly lowered her down. As he lowered her, he brought her body close to his and slid her down his body.

Rose took a deep breath and held it, the fear of his feeling the revolver was all she could think of now. Then she felt the revolver dig into her skin. Rose wanted to scream. She was in agony. He stood holding her for what seemed forever. Then her feet were on the ground, and the discomfort eased up.

To Rose's amazement he was gentle. For a minute their eyes met. Rose thought the icy stare was gone. She noticed the color of his eyes for the first time. They were dark brown. With the sun shining into them, she had this feeling he was reading her mind.

He took her hand and led her to the water hole. Rose splashed water on her face. Then cupped her hands to drink. She knew he was holding the rein in one hand and filling his two water canteens but she could feel his eyes on her.

Rose had not seen his face up to this time. His bandana had remained on.

She was not aware that while she was drinking he had removed the bandana. In an instant, time stood still for her. It was five years ago. This was the face she had seen when she crawled out of the water from her private inlet at Joseph's.

Rose's body became rigid . All of her muscles tightened up. This was not possible. Had he been looking for her all of this time? Could this just be fate?

He looked into her eyes. Rose did not know for sure if he had recognized her. She quickly turned her face away.

Rose knew her escape had to be soon, swift, and accurate. She could not make any mistakes.

Joseph had always told her if she was in trouble, be quiet and listen to every word. Never argue. Look into his eyes at all times. But what if he knew who she was.

Rose thought about the time in the cabin when the robbers broke in. She shot the revolver but missed the man's foot on purpose. This was a time she would not miss.

⤳ Chapter 7 ⤳

The man spoke, " We need to hurry. The sky looks full. We're in for a bad storm."

He placed her back on the saddle and pulled himself up behind her. He again slipped his arm around her. He leaned his body against her and held her tightly.

Rose was aware of the direction they were heading. It was toward a dense wooded area. He was right about a storm coming. The sky looked threatening. The clouds were hanging low and looked dark and rolling in the sky.

The thunder and lightening were making the horse jumpy. They rode into the trees. It was dangerous to ride with the strong winds. The tree limbs were moving in every direction, striking them, tearing at their clothes, and scratching their faces.

He suddenly yelled, "We need to walk from here."

He got off first, then helped her down. The rain had started. It was an instant torrent of water.

He took his bed roll off his horse, unwrapped it to make a shelter for them. He insisted she put on his poncho. They sat on his bed roll on the ground under thick bushes with his blanket wrapped around them both. She tried to keep a small distance between them but that was almost impossible.

Rose leaned back against the nearest tree trunk and closed her eyes while the rain continued to pour. She was still wondering if he had recognized her, and most of all, where was he taking her?

The storm would not let her escape tonight. She would have nowhere to hide before he caught her.

When Rose awoke in the morning, she was alone under the blanket. The odor of coffee and wet firewood drifted toward her. She quickly threw the blanket off and stood up, knowing the man was watching her.

He handed her a cup of hot coffee and a piece of beef jerky. She had not eaten since leaving the train.

She asked if she could step into the trees for a minute. He did not answer, just motioned for her to go. She went in far enough so he could not see her. When she stood up, she looked around. Getting lost meant nothing to her for she had no idea where she was, or what direction was where.

Rose lifted her coat and dress up. She darted in one direction, and then turned and tried to run in another. The trees, bushes, and weeds were all matted together, making it difficult to hurry.

The rain had turned the solid ground into mud. Her boots were covered with heavy mud. The bottom of her beautiful black wool coat was covered with sand burs. The soft fur collar that had snuggly fit up around her neck was wet, and lay limp, crushed in spots. Seeds from the wet weeds stuck to it.

Suddenly, she heard the limbs breaking behind her, and she knew he was coming after her. Beside her was a large broken tree limb. Rose knew she could not out run him, so her first instinct was to hide. She crawled in under the limb as far as she could get in the wet, tall grass.

She tried hard not even to breath.

The noise was getting closer. The horse was breaking off branches, and she could hear his hooves hitting the ground. The other sound she heard was the man swearing in Spanish, and he sounded enraged.

Rose held her breath, thinking he would shoot her when he found her. She heard the horse stop. Nothing moved. He was listening for her.

When Rose heard the horse move she, had to breath. It sounded so loud. She thought the man could hear her. The horse was walking further away. She remained under the log most of the morning.

⌒ Chapter 8 ⌒

She opened her eyes and watched a bug, and when it appeared to come toward her, she wanted to scream. Instead she closed her eyes again. The birds overhead sounded so happy and carefree. She wished she could be a bird and feel that way. She would just fly away.

Rose was sure the man was franticly searching for her. He knew she had not gone far, and Rose was sure he would find her. And this time he would tie her up. This was not a man to cross in any way.

The ground was becoming extremely hard and uncomfortable to lie on without being able to move any part of her body.

She wondered if she moved further under the large limb, she could get out on the other side. Then she would go in a different direction. Rose moved an inch at a time. Now she was laying directly under the log. She began to feel the need for more air. She needed to get out.

Rose found her legs would not fit. She needed to dig some dirt out as her legs could not move away from the log. She reached down as far as her hand could reach and began to dig in the dirt, small amounts at a time.

Rose continued to dig, and then she would move one leg to see if both legs would fit under the log. She found she could move her legs, even if it meant tearing the skin off of her knees. She was free, and on the opposite side of the log. Very slowly, she moved over on her stomach.

Raising her head to see how she could get away from this area. The trees over head were filled with large birds. They took flight, while extending and flapping their huge wings. At the same time they were making squealing high pitched bird noises. The sound paralyzed her with fear.

The noise sent Rose rolling back under the log and she lay motionless. Just as she suspected, she heard limbs snapping off as the man tried to get through the overgrown mass of brush.

Rose lay listening as the horse came within a few feet of her. She turned her head as far as she could, her ear close to the ground. She tried to listen for the horse's hooves to move away. Minutes went by, and then she heard the horse move. Rose heard the hooves step down, crushing leaves, weeds and twigs. The underbrush was thick. The man was moving away.

Chapter 9

It was not going to be possible to try to move until dark. She closed her eyes but her mind would not rest. A voice in her mind kept saying over and over, remember the story. Rose, remember the story I told you. Joseph had told her so many pioneer stories as a young man homesteading in 1840 with his father and mother.

She loved to hear his stories. It was several minutes before Rose could think of the story. Joseph told Rose how his father staked out 3,000 acres of land. Then made the trip on his horse, sometimes riding, sometimes walking, for his horse was old. He made the trip into Oklahoma City to claim his land.

Now all of that land belonged to her. No one was going to take the land away from her. Least of all a man who steals, and one who commits a crime against another human being.

Joseph had described his father as a good, caring man. His renters all needed a cabin to live in and barns for their animals. The first years after he rented his land out, he helped each family build a home.

It was after each family was busy with children, crops and their livestock. They would work late and go to bed tired from the long days. During the night hours and early morning, someone was visiting each farmstead. The person was very clever. He would sneak to one farm one night, and then wait a few nights and watch till all the lamps were out. He would quietly creep into another renter's homestead.

Joseph told Rose, each renter made the trip to his father's homestead and told him how they were missing chickens and eggs. They came to ask for help to catch the thief.

Joseph said, "A trap was set." Each renter took his turn staying up all night, waiting. The thief was tied up securely and made to walk down Main street in town behind the horse of the man he had stolen from.

Rose thought, what a good idea. How could a young woman set a trap? She felt so helpless but she had to try. Setting a trap for a man twice her size. A man who had a horse. A man who felt no shame when he hurt others.

It was becoming dark, and the wind blew the limbs and leaves making it spooky. Rose did not know where he was camping but she was sure he wasn't far. She thought if he had made a campfire she could smell the smoke. Also she thought, maybe the horse would make some noises, warning her where he was.

Rose moved slowly out from under the log. The noises in the forest made her jumpy. She could hear an owl off in the distance. She could hear many different noises. It was a mixture of birds, bugs, and animals.Rose felt they were protective sounds. The animals were moving, making noises. The man would not know if it was her or something else.

One step at a time, making her way was very difficult. She went in the direction she thought the horse was moving when the man had heard the birds take flight over her earlier in the morning.

She had her hands out in front of her, feeling her way, trying to move the limbs without making any noise. Her coat was wet and felt heavy. But it kept the limbs from scratching her arms.

Her hair was hanging loose, down to her waist. It was full of snarls and caught on the branches. When it caught, she had to stop and untwist it from a branch. Her hands were scratched as was her face. Rose was in pain, and her skin was burning. But no amount of pain would stop her now.

Chapter 10

It was time to find a limb. Something she could handle easy. It would have to be hard and firm. Rose got down and felt around on the ground. She found a few, but this limb had to be just right. She crawled several more feet and then she found one. Her hand reach out and grabbed it firmly.

Rose felt sure this was her only chance to be free of this man. She was not going to let him belittle her anymore.

She had crawled over trees laying in her path. She had pulled apart large bushes to crawl through.

The smoke she could smell was of a fire smoldering, so she hoped he was asleep for the night. Rose was getting close. The horse moved, making her realize how near she was.

Rose wanted to get behind his head. She stopped, the fear of the night, the complete darkness, the fear of failing suddenly engulfing her. Then a thought came to her. Both John and her father were waiting for her in Oklahoma City.

She was on her hands and knees straining to see his camp. The first thing she could see was the eyes of the horse. He was looking in her direction. Usually, a rider would lay a few feet away in front of his horse. She turned and moved around the large tree. The man was lying under and next to it. She could hear him inhale and exhale.

Rose needed to rouse him so he would sit up. She could see the outline of the saddle. He was lying with his head on it.

With her hands shaking, she raised the limb, tapped the saddle. The man jerked up his head. Rose slammed the limb down on the back of the man's head. He made a cry of pain and fell down immediately.

She removed his gun first and put it in her coat pocket. Rose knew where to look for the rope, it had been on the side of the saddle, when she was forced off of the train. She groped around in the darkness until she found it.

She turned the man over. He was limp. She hoped he was still alive. One hand at a time, she tied the rope around each wrist. Then she wrapped the rope around the man's neck, then back down around his waist. She tied a knot around his waist, and left the long end of the rope to tie on the saddle.

The saddle blanket was rolled up and laying on the saddle for the man's head to lay on. Rose laid the blanket on the horse. She swung the saddle up over his back, then reached under the horse, feeling to grab the strap to cinch the saddle up tight. She crawled around on the ground until she found the bridle and slipped the bit into the horse's mouth. Rose pushed the strap up over the horse's ears and threw the reins up and over the saddle horn.

Rose was ready.

One canteen was full, the other had a small amount in it. Rose drank, then poured the rest over the man's head. He coughed and woke swearing in Spanish. She needed him up and on his feet.

Without getting close to him, Rose untied the horse and climbed up onto the saddle with the full canteen. It was a relief to see the morning sun making a small amount of light come through the trees. It was just enough to start on the trail back from this horrible captivity.

She pulled gently on one rein to move the horse a few feet. The man struggled to stand. Slowly they began to move in the direction she hoped was how they had entered the tree area.

Rose tried to block out the outbursts coming from the man behind her.

Because the limbs could knock her off the horse, Rose laid her head on the horse's mane.

Chapter 11

As the sun rose, the flashing of the bright light between the trees made it almost impossible to see at times. Rose spent most of the time looking back at the man. He stumbled many times. Rose would stop until he got back on his feet.

He continued swearing at her in Spanish. Then he was yelling, "Stop, stop," She turned to see the man on the ground. Without her knowing, he had fallen and was being dragged. Blood was running down his cheek.

She tugged on the reins for the horse to stop. The man did not get up. Rose waited, not wanting to go near him. She knew she could not trust him.

She was sure the trail she had picked was right. Rose shouted back at him, "The water hole is near. You can wash off there."

He slowly got up on his knees first, and then up on his feet. She could tell by the look on his face, it was an effort on his part. She could also tell he was a very angry man.

They arrived at the water hole. Rose rode the horse into the water. The man followed, and dropped to his knees in the water. He put his face into the water to drink and to cleanse the wound on his face.

While the man was on his knees, Rose dismounted quickly and filled the empty canteen. She mounted the horse, and urged the horse out of the water. The man was again pulled to his feet. He looked tired. Nothing had changed, except now, he was swearing at her in English.

Rose was making plans in her mind. She remembered the end of the tree area was close. But she needed to stay in the tree area that night because with the end of the rope that she had, she would tie him to a tree.

Carefully she planned when she would stop and make camp. A tree of medium size was needed to tie the man to. The sun was starting to go down. In this vast thickness of trees and brush it would be dark long before the sun was completely out of sight.

Rose found a tree that the rope would wrap around at least two times. She rode the horse as close to the tree as she could get him. She stepped down off the horse with the rope in her hand, keeping the horse between them. Rose wrapped the rope around the tree and stepped back, pulling, so the man came up to the tree. She walked around the tree one more time, always keeping the horse close so the man could not bump her or fall on her on purpose. This night the man was going to have to sleep standing up.

The saddle bag had several strips of beef jerky left in it. She pulled a strip apart so she had several small pieces. Rose put it into a coffee cup that she had taken from the saddle bag. She stood as far away from him as she could and put the cup to his mouth. She did this several times as he had not eaten all day. She then poured the water into the cup from the canteen, and he drank several cups.

He stared at her. His dark eyes never turned away. Finally, with broken accent, speaking slowly, not like his swear words, he said, "You are the girl from Oklahoma." He had known all along who she was.

Rose was stunned. "What are you doing here? Did you follow me from Joseph Higgins' cabin? Did you ride to St. Louis to find me? Why? Why?" she asked franticly.

Rose thought the wicked smile on his face could not hide the deceit in his heart.

"Lady, you belong to me. You are so beautiful," he said without hesitation.

Rose was so startled. It took a few minutes before she responded. She wanted to call him by his name. But this man would always remain nameless to Rose.

"Sir," Rose began, with urgency to convince him how wrong he was. "You have intruded on my life. I do not belong to you. I will never belong to you. You cannot take something that does not belong to you." Rose had no intention of mentioning John's name in case this man ever met up with him.

She told him, "I am obligated to return and take care of my blind father."

He continued to glare without blinking his eyes. He said, "Someday soon, you will be mine." This man had ignored everything she had told him. Rose decided she needed to get as far away from this man as she could. If she got on the horse this instant she could be to the train tracks by evening.

Rose turned away and pictured in her mind what this man would look like if she left him tied there, and did not return. The birds and animals would leave nothing of him but his bones.

Rose knew she could not do it.

⌒ Chapter 12 ⌒

Rose turned and walked the horse away from him. She walked straight in the opposite direction than the man faced. She found a place of rocks and overgrowth to hide in. She would go back for him in the morning and find him without getting lost.

This man was nothing like Joseph Higgins had been or like John Fitzpatrick.

The sounds of the forest and the thoughts of this detestable man made the night long and fearful for Rose. The morning would be relief for her because she was heading to Oklahoma City.

All Rose had to do was go back to the tree, untie the man, and they would be starting back. It was close to morning before Rose fell into a deep sleep. When she woke, she felt disoriented and almost confused. In a few minutes it was all straight in her mind, and she needed to hurry.

Saddling the horse and repacking the saddlebag took only a short time. Rose headed back in a straight line like she had planned. As she got near, she dismounted, and led the horse up to the back of the tree. She was sure this was the right area and the right tree.

But something looked different. She started around the tree to untie him. She opened her mouth and the air she took in made her cough and choke. The disbelief first, then the realization of what she was not seeing, suddenly set in.

The man was gone. Only a small piece of the rope lay on the ground. Rose quickly picked up the rope and could see it had been cut with a knife.

Rose had missed finding the knife he had been hiding. She had only taken his gun.

Wasting no time, she knew she had to get back to the clearing and try to get to the train tracks. She would follow the train tracks to Oklahoma.

Pulling the reins, she tried to make the horse run. Rose started back in the direction of the clearing. She tripped several times, nearly falling to the ground that was covered with years of vegetated debris. The horse would step, and at times throw his head upward, as if trying to keep his balance.

The clearing was up ahead. Rose mounted the horse, fearing the man would jump out at her. When she was out in the open, she pressed the horse's belly with the stirrups, and the horse was in a full gallop.

Going back to the train tracks when they were first stopped by the robbers would be a waste of time. So Rose tried to picture in her mind where the train would be now. It had been two whole days.

The horse continued running until she felt the man could not have gotten that far. She slowed him down for they had a long way to go.

Off in the distance, Rose thought she could see a small settlement. But the man could have made it there. She would not ride near it.

She would have to share her canteen of water with the horse. She did not know of any water hole. The sky was so clear and blue, and the rye grass she was in, waved back and forth with the wind. The only sounds were birds flying above and the rustling noise as the horse moved through the tall grass.

After what seemed like hours, Rose dismounted and let the horse stand, rest and eat grass. He had had very little to eat since this dreadful excursion had started. She opened a canteen and lifted his head up as far as she could, and slowly poured water along the inside of his mouth. He jerked his head up and down and she would try again.

Chapter 13

In the next few hours only the land changed. It became rolling with ditches and small drop off-cliffs. The horse was walking. Rose was trying to look ahead and pick the best path. This would slow her down.

The terrain she found herself in was deep, but more level for the horse to walk on. She let the horse walk at the pace he wanted.

The horse's ears came up, at the same time Rose heard a horse whinny. Rose stopped the horse, and crawled off and held the reins, and pulled the horse's head close to her chest. She stood very still.

Rose thought she could hear several horses. They were coming closer. But they were traveling up higher on a ledge. As they got closer, Rose could hear voices speaking in Spanish.

She closed her eyes and prayed they would not see her. The horses continued on past her. She wondered if they could be part of the man's men.

Rose stood leaning on this long-legged, large horse that was almost human. He followed instructions as if he could understand English. He was gentle and tame. She wondered how the man could own a beautiful creature like this, unless he was a horse thief, too. It also occurred to her he would never let her keep this beautiful horse.

Rose thought the horse needed to stop for the night as much as she did. This ravine would be the best place for them. She found a large stone sticking out along the bank and wrapped the halter strap around it. She thought he was as relieved as she was when she took the saddle off.

The many nights without sleep had caught up with her. She felt safe with this hiding place. She woke up long after the sun had risen. The horse stood patiently waiting to get saddled up. She knew she had to get out of this dry stony area. No grass could grow here. Rose looked for a path to get to the surface.

With Rose holding on tightly, the horse with his strong body, dug in and walked straight up to a ledge leading them to a level of different land. It took most of the morning to get out of this rugged area. The horse was as determined as she was.

Rose could see what looked like a valley. When they got closer, they found they were in a lush grassy plain with few trees. The horse could eat before going any further. She again tried to give him a little water. Rose had one beef jerky strip left. She broke a small piece off. This would have to last until she made it to a homestead.

Rose tied the reins around the saddle horn. She took the rope off the saddle, tied one end to the bridle and the other to a tree, giving the horse room to walk and eat. She removed the bed blanket and laid it on the ground. Rose laid down. Her body was in pain from riding for two days.

She had not had a bath since leaving her father's home. Her hair was snarled and matted together. Her beautiful clothes were dirty and torn, with bits and pieces of weeds sticking to them. But she was free.

She drifted off to sleep thinking about swimming in Joseph's creek. When she woke, the sun was covered with clouds of threatening rain. She needed to travel as far as she could before the sun set for the night.

Chapter 14

The horse was always ready to go. Rose had many miles to travel. She thought if the horse could stand to travel 30 miles a day, they could get to Oklahoma City in three weeks.

Rose prepared for making a few more miles before dark. She hoped to find shelter when she stopped for the night. The horse acted as if he sensed something. He was impatient, his back hooves pranced back and forth. He had not done this before. She grabbed the saddle horn and had one foot in the stirrup, and he was moving.

At first, Rose tried to hold him back because of the long distance they had to go. Then she loosened the reins, and let him run like he wanted. She could feel the power of his muscles under her as he left one mile at a time behind them.

The sound of thunder and then the streak of lightening were ahead of her. They were heading into it. When the lighting lit up the sky she looked in every direction for some kind of shelter. In one of the flashes, she saw a building.

Rose did not know what it was but the rain started. It was coming with a driving force. It took only a short time and she was wet and trembling from the cold, soaking rain.

Rose put her head down and just hung on. The horse slowed down as he approached the building. The darkness lit up with the lightening, and she could see a door. She slipped off the horse and opened the door.

With the door open, she could see a stall. She led the horse to it tied him to the manger, and removed the saddle. Her heavy, wet clothing was cold, and her body began to shiver. She removed her heavy coat. Rose found another stall with hay and grain, and fed the horse and wiped him off with the saddle blanket.

Rose took the sleeping blanket and spread it out in the grain stall. She closed the barn door and felt her way back to the blanket.

Rose knew she was sick. She closed her eyes thinking of John and her father.

Rose felt so cold, and yet her body was burning. She had not eaten since she and her father ate together from the sack lunch on the train. She had eaten a beef jerky once a day to stay alive. The water she drank had been a very small amount because she shared her water with the horse.

Chapter 15

Rose was trying to wake up. She had such a strange feeling. She thought she could hear someone moaning, and then she realized it was her. But why? Where was she? She heard voices, then she thought she was being lifted up into the air. Someone was carrying her.

She knew she needed to start again. She tried. The horse needed to be saddled. Nothing was making sense. Then she slipped back into a deep sleep.

Rose slowly opened her eyes. What she saw was alarming. She closed her eyes quickly. Then she opened them again. The eyes staring back at her were all around her. She looked at each set of eyes. Each set of eyes had a small head. They were all little in size.

Then someone walked up close to her and said, "Are you awake?" It sounded like a woman, the voice was soft and gentle.

Rose was trying to answer her. Then the voice said, "You've been very sick. When my husband found you, you had a very high fever. I wish you could tell us your name, where you came from, and where you are going. This is not a safe area for a young woman to be traveling alone in."

Rose opened her mouth, and all that came out, in a shaky voice was "I'm heading for Oklahoma City. My horse."

Rose heard her say, "Your horse is fine."

Then the voice said, "She has to rest now children, let's leave her sleep." Rose closed her eyes, and felt something good had just happened but she didn't know what.

The sun was shining in on her face when she woke the next morning. Her eyes were open, and she looked the room over. It was clean and warm. She saw her clothes hanging over a chair.

They looked clean and dry. This was not the barn stall but how did she get here? Rose was wearing a flannel night gown. The bed had a straw mattress, just like the one on her bed in St. Louis. She was covered with a patch quilt, like the quilt on her childhood bed.

Her mind was so tired, and she was trying to clear all of this up. She pulled the patch quilt over her head to block out the sun. Rose heard a noise and she slowly lowered her quilt. A little girl stood beside her bed looking down at her.

The girl said, "Would you like me to read to you?"

Rose whispered, "Yes."

The girl then told Rose the name of the books she had, "I have two books. One is called, *Columbus Discovers America* and the other is, *George Washington's Dentures*"

Before the girl began to read, the room filled up with children of all ages. They all gathered around her bed. There were so many, Rose tried to count them. One little boy crawled up on her bed, and gently touched her face, then he leaned over and kissed her forehead.

Rose began to cry. The tears welled up in her eyes and streamed down her cheeks. The memories of her kissing Joseph each night after she had read to him came to her.

She had no idea the impact of her tears on these children. Every child had tears. The boys tried to hide theirs but the girls were touched so deeply. One of the older girls took the end of her apron and gently wiped Rose's tears dry.

Rose wanted to tell them why she had cried but she did not have strength to talk. In an emotional voice, she asked the girl to read, "Columbus Discovers America." She had read it to Joseph many evenings.

The young girl held the book up so Rose could see the pictures. The girl read every page but she had the words memorized. Rose looked at her and judged her to be 10 years old, and she could not read.

Closing her eyes, Rose was saddened to think of all this young girl was missing out on. She was asleep as this unconcerned girl finished talking about the last picture.

When she woke again, all of the children were on their knees around her bed. A little boy sat next to her head with his little hand on her hair. Rose looked around her bed. She counted five children on each side of her. Then the little boy on her bed, and then the girl reading the pictures in her book. That was 12, but then she thought, maybe, she was seeing double.

The children were all clean and well mannered. Did they all belong to this kind woman? Was this all one family? The girl's dresses were all made out of flour sacks as well as the boy's shirts.

Chapter 16

Rose was close to being in a deep sleep but she could hear a voice saying, "Mother, are you going to tell her about the man who stopped and asked about her?"

Then she heard the kind voice say, "No, we will not tell her until she is stronger. I'm glad your father hid her horse, because he wanted to look in our barn."

After everyone left her room, Rose tried to get out of bed. She moved the quilt and moved her legs to the edge of the bed, then put her feet on the floor. She was sitting up for the first time. The room seemed to be moving. If only she could get to her clothes. They were only a few feet away. Rose was trying to stand up. With her here, this family was not safe.

She heard loud voices outside of her door. Rose sat back down on her bed and then laid down while pulling up the patch quilt over her.

The door opened and several of the children came hurrying in. One was a young man, she had not seen before. He acted very polite as he said, "Madam, we need to move you. We have an attic, you'll have to allow me to take you there."

Rose was hysterical, "Why? Why?"

"Madam," the young man said softly, "We believe you are going to be kidnapped. There is a man who keeps coming back here asking about you. Please do not make any noise."

He slipped his arms under her, lifted her up out of the bed. The girl who had read to Rose, immediately went to the chair and grabbed Rose's clothes, she lifted the patch quilt, and laid them at the foot of the bed, under the quilt. The young girl then crawled into the bed.

The young man carried Rose into another bedroom. He went to the closet. Another child was there to open the closet door. The child pushed the clothes that were hanging there to one side. A ladder leading up the wall to the ceiling was exposed. He moved to the steps leading up into the attic. Rose put her arms around his neck, making it easier for him to climb the steps. He had no problem carrying her up the steps as she had lost a great amount of weight.

He laid her on a blanket that was already laying on the floor. He covered her with another blanket. They had a small space as the attic had a trunk and a few pieces of old furniture in it.

The trap door was closed and locked. The child in the bedroom below then pushed the clothes back to hide the ladder.

The air in the attic was stale and dry. It also smelled musty. It had no windows so it was extremely dark.

The quiet young man sat down beside her and held her hand. Suddenly they could hear voices. It was not the soft voices she had heard since arriving here but a loud, angry voice. The man was in the house searching for her.

Rose reached for the young man to hold her. He moved to be closer and to hold her in his arms. Her whole body was trembling. His strong arms encircled her, and he whispered in her ear, "He will never get to you. My family will protect you."

Rose had no idea who she was with, and why this wonderful family chose to risk letting this violent man invade their home. She had plunged them into a situation they knew nothing about, and they knew nothing about her. They had cared for her during her illness, and now they were protecting her with their lives.

The loud talking faded. They did not know if the man had left the house. They were at a disadvantage not knowing if everyone was safe. She had not planned for anything like this to happen. Rose would never have intentionally hurt any member of this family.

⮞ Chapter 17 ⮜

The young man again whispered in her ear saying, "I'll wait awhile before opening the trap door. The plan is that one of my family will tap on the trap door when it is safe to go back down."

Rose needed to know what was going on in this house so she began by asking how she got into the house from the barn.

The young man answered saying, "My name is Henry, and I'm the one who carried you into our home. My father found you sleeping in the barn. You have been sick for three days. My mother has nursed you day and night. She brought your fever down and spoon fed you broth. My sisters have taken turns sitting by your bed."

Henry said one more thing, "A woman does not travel alone in these parts unless they are in some kind of trouble. Are you in trouble?"

Rose lay with her eyes closed, and her head on his chest listening. She finally answered, "It's such a long story. When I am completely well, I will tell you everything."

"Now," Rose said, "I just want to know about your family. You see, I was raised alone. I have no brothers or sisters. The only family I have is my father, and he is waiting for me in Oklahoma City. I must get there to take care of him. I'm leaving as soon as I can ride."

"Please, tell me your name first," he said, "Then I will tell you about my family."

"My name is Rose, Rose Donlin. I hope no one in your family gets hurt because of me," as her voice trailed off.

Henry told her, "I have 13 brothers and sisters. The four other children are children of my mother's sister. My aunt had been sick for a long time, and when she died, my mother insisted we take her children and raise them. Now, our family numbers 18 children, plus our father and mother. I am the oldest."

For a few minutes neither spoke. They sat in the darkness in silence.

Henry spoke first, "Rose, you have a beautiful name."

Rose couldn't speak. She remembered John saying the very same thing to her.

Henry told her how all of the children wanted to help take care of her. The girls bathed her and washed her long hair. How they had dressed her cuts with salve.

Rose said, "I don't remember. How did they bathe me, and especially wash my hair?"

"The girls locked all of the boys out of the house, including me." Henry told her. "Then they carried the tub into your bedroom, filled it with warm water they had heated on the stove. My mother, and six of my sisters put you into the tub the first day you were here. You were cut and bruised. The cuts needed to be washed and cleaned. Each of my sisters took turns feeding you."

Rose was overwhelmed by all of this information. She asked Henry, "How can I ever repay your family?"

"No one should ever be treated the way you must have been." Henry told her. "My family wanted only to save you."

A tap on the trap door from down below indicated they could come down from the attic.

The family was all waiting for them as Henry carried Rose down the ladder. Henry took Rose to the kitchen where Henry's father was waiting. She got to see each of the members of this wonderful family.

Rose's first impression of Henry's father was his firmness, and he looked strong. His jaw was set with determination. She noticed how quiet it was, no one was talking. It was as if everyone was waiting for him to speak.

He looked directly at Rose and said, "I believe that man knows you are here. We need to sneak you out after dark. We will walk you out. Henry will have your horse ready and will meet you a few miles from here. Henry will accompany you to Oklahoma City. He will take care of you and keep this man from finding you. I will give your guns to you when you are ready to leave our home. I believe you need to change the way you look. One of my sons can let you have a pair of overalls, a shirt, and work boots. Also a hat will help keep the man from seeing your hair. Now, we need to hurry so you can get an early start."

Henry's father walked to Rose, took her hand and kissed it, and then left to help get her horse ready. She knew he was right to take the danger away from his family. He showed what a wonderful father he was.

The older girls helped Rose dress like a boy. What they didn't expect her to do was ask for a sharp knife. She held her long hair out away from her head and began cutting all of her hair off. The girls stood in silence watching as Rose's beautiful long hair fell in a heap on the floor. This was an act of desperation.

Chapter 18

The family did not watch as Rose slipped out the back door in the darkness. If the man was near, they wanted nothing unusual for him to see. They all sat at the supper table with the lamp low so the room was almost dark. They all sat in their usual places but no one talked.

Rose had been told exactly where Henry would be waiting with her horse. Henry was right where he was suppose to be. He sat on his horse with the reins of Rose's horse in his hand. She knew she would be late. She tried to hurry but was completely out of breath when she got to her horse.

Rose stood and leaned up against the big horse to rest. It was as if he knew it was her, and he never moved.

Henry slid off his horse, lifted her up onto the saddle, handed her the reins, and returned to his horse. Henry moved out first, and Rose followed close.

The heaven was filled with stars. The night was calm and quiet, and the air was warm. If this was of different circumstances, it would have been an enjoyable night to ride horseback . They traveled most of the night on his father's land. Henry knew the area well. He motioned for Rose to pull up beside him. He was concerned if she could ride the rest of the night.

Rose told him, "I can do this."

The silhouette of Henry astride his horse, in the dark in front of her, gave her a feeling of comfort and safety. He rode tall and straight, and she could see his broad frame.

He had been so kind to her when they were in the attic alone together. She thought he was a good man like Joseph Higgins.

A tiny amount of light was coming up in the east. Henry told her his plan was that they would make it to a creek he knew of. The horses needed water. He thought they could ride till noon. Then they would camp in a hidden area, that way he could keep her safe. They would rest until darkness and start again.

Henry also mentioned the territory they were in. He had not traveled here before.

At times, they rode side by side. Henry glanced at her several times, thinking about how beautiful she was. But he also thought something about her looked different.

Henry set the pace, keeping the horses at a cantor. If the man was on foot, Henry thought they could get ahead of him.

The creek was a welcome sight for Henry, Rose, and the horses. They led the horses to an area of the bank that the horses could stand and drink. They found a secluded area to camp in. Henry laid his blanket close to hers because he needed her close to protect her.

Rose removed her hat before laying down. Henry drew in his breath as he looked at what used to be a lovely head of long hair. Rose was aware he was stunned by what he was seeing.

Rose spoke slowly, "Henry, I needed to cut off my hair. I needed to help protect you and your family. I hoped he would not recognize me if he saw me."

Rose continued, "No one knows how cruel this man is. He has been waiting and watching for me a long time. He thinks he owns me."

Henry moved on his blanket to be closer to her. His body was laying close enough so his shoulder and arm were lightly touching her.

Rose looked up at the bright shining stars and wondered why she felt a desire to lie next to Henry and why she trusted him so completely. She had not felt this peaceful for a very long time.

❧ Chapter 19 ❧

Rose's mind wondered back to when she lived in the cabin with Joseph. The first year she learned what hard work was. She learned how strong she was. Nothing was easy. The meals she prepared were meat from the smoke house, vegetables from the fruit cave, and lard that was stored in the cool cave. Fresh biscuits were made each day for breakfast and bread was made every day. Flour and sugar were kept in tin cans in the cabin to prevent bugs and weevils getting in them. She carried all of the water from the creek.

Rose woke to hearing a sound she had to listen close to hear. The morning noises of birds, ducks on the creek were mixed with another sound. Henry was whistling. What a joy it was to hear. She was feeling this was a new beginning. The bad times were all behind her.

The coffee and breakfast Henry prepared were a wonderful way to start their day of travel. Nothing was left behind for anyone to recognize this as a camp. Henry carried limbs, sticks and any other debris to hide the campsite.

The horses acted ready to start. They emerged out of the tree and creek area. They realized they were out in an open route where they could be seen easily from all sides. It was a rough, hilly uneven region, with no trees to hide in. Small streams flowed in washed- out gullies. The horses stepped into the water with no fear and lifted their legs high to hurry up the bank.

The only other forms of life were small animals that scurried down into holes in the ground. Birds flew straight up into the air when the horses frightened them from their hiding place in the tall weeds.

By late in the afternoon, the air was changing. It was cooling off. Henry slowed down to let Rose ride up beside him. Henry reached over to untie her blanket from behind her saddle. He unfolded it and wrapped it around her shoulders. Rose sat watching him lean over her and tuck the blanket around her body. He overlapped it around her chest.

Henry's face was close to her. She wanted him close, and she didn't know why she felt that way.

Rose whispered, "Thank you, Henry." He only smiled and winked at her.

He returned to his place in front of her. As they moved on, the land flattened out, and Henry was aware of what he was seeing ahead of them. The barbed wire fence was what ranchers were using to keep their range cattle in. He wanted to make sure they were on the outside of the fence because ranchers were always looking for cattle rustlers. So, getting caught inside of some rancher's barbed wire fence could mean a beating or death.

Rose suddenly jerked on the reins to stop her horse as panic set in, at what she saw coming toward them. Henry turned his horse around and pulled up next to her. He had seen the lone rider coming toward them, too. Henry reached in his saddle bag and handed Rose her revolver.

He also pulled out the gun Rose had taken from the man.

Henry said, "We cannot out run him. We need to only use our gun if this is the man, and if he tries to take you. Keep your hat low on your head and keep your head down."

Henry positioned his horse sideways in front of her to shield her.

Under Rose's blanket her hands were clasped together holding the revolver, and her finger was on the trigger. She was waiting and expecting the worst, and she was not going to hesitate.

Henry sat on his horse ready to do whatever he had to do to protect Rose. He was an honorable, determined man.

The lone rider was coming at a full gallop. Rose strained her eyes to see his size, his hair color and most of all if he had dark eyes.

Henry did not know what the man looked like but he was prepared to decide in an instant what to do.

It took a few minutes, and the rider pulled his horse up in front of Henry. Henry quickly turned his head and shot a look at Rose. The look on her face told him, this was not the man.

The rider spoke first saying, "Get off of this land as fast as you can. The boss has had some cattle disappear. He will shoot anyone on his land."

Henry's boots touched his horse, and his horse leaped into a gallop. Henry's only concern was to keep Rose safe.

Rose sat in a daze, unable to move. She had come so close to pulling the trigger of her revolver. Her fear of the man could have taken the life of an innocent man. It would have been a senseless killing. She decided her thought of imprisonment had to stop. She was going to have to face the man.

Rose looked at the young rider. He was just a boy. He didn't even have facial hair yet. His body was small, his feet didn't touch the stirrups. She thought this could have ended so tragically.

Chapter 20

Henry stopped his horse and waited for Rose to catch up to him. Whenever they could, they rode side by side the rest of the day. The trees and hills made the ride slow at times. They didn't get as many miles behind them as they had hoped for.

The darkness made it hard to travel. The night air felt damp and heavy. Henry knew she was cold and tired. He told her, "It shouldn't be long, and we'll be at the lake my father told me about. We'll camp there tonight."

The closer they got to the lake, they realized they were riding into a thick cover of fog. Henry moved his horse close to Rose.

Rose could see a campfire burning brightly through the fog. She could hear voices of several men talking. Henry pulled on the reins to keep from getting too near the other men. He wanted to get a distance away so he could be alone with Rose. He wanted to take care of her. He found it was not going to be easy, riding along the edge of the lake.

They came upon more campsites with five or six men talking and drinking. At times the men were loud and sounded angry. Henry was leading her, moving along, they could see more glowing embers through the fog.

Henry's voice sounded worried, "We have to water our horses, Rose. After that, we need to ride away from the lake. It's not safe for us."

Henry found an open spot that they could lead the horses down to drink. They needed to refill their canteens because he did not know when they would find water again.

The campsite they found was a short distance from the lake. The fog surrounded them. It was cold but Henry was adamant about his decision not to start a fire. Henry felt they could rest without being found.

The horses were taken care of first, then Henry laid the blankets together on the ground, they covered with the horse blankets. Falling asleep came easy.

Rose woke with the brutal knowledge she was being suffocated. Someone had their hand over her face. Then she heard a low whisper in her ear. "Don't make a sound. Someone has found us. I saw a light. It looks like a man carrying a lantern coming this way. Come with me to get the horses ready."

Henry grabbed the blankets in one hand, and took Rose's hand in the other and headed toward the horses.

They had the horses nearly ready when they both heard a man's voice say, "What's your hurry?"

Henry answered with a bold loud voice, "My brother and I have to get home. Our mother is sick. So, if you don't mind, we'll be on our way."

"Brother. We thought you might have a girl with you." The stranger said with disappointment in his voice.

Chapter 21

The next couple hours they rode in silence, then the sun seem to bring some relief with the light. Riding behind Henry's horse for endless miles, Rose noticed the grass was no longer green. It was sagebrush, and hundreds of grasshoppers were jumping up with every hoof movement of the horses.

It looked dry. It was dusty, and hard to breath. Henry motioned for her to put the end of her blanket over her mouth and nose. The dead grass made a crushing sound. Rose thought the trees looked dead as they passed them. Grasshoppers flew off of the trees hitting them and the horses. The leaves of all of the trees had been eaten by the grasshoppers.

Rose's mind drifted off thinking about and remembering the fire at Joseph's renter. They had not received rain that year, and it was dry like this area. Joseph had told her he thought they had more grasshoppers than usual, and each day brought more when the rain did not come.

The grasshoppers ate everything in her garden. They ate the grass and weeds, then started on the tree leaves. They ate bark off of the trees, killing the young trees. Joseph insisted they stay in the cabin when they saw swarms of the insects flying through the sky. The sky looked dark at times. They could hear the grasshoppers hitting the cabin.

Rose remembered doing chores early in the morning and doing more of her evening chores at that time, too. She tried to keep all of the animals locked in the barn during the heat of the day when the grasshoppers were jumping on them. Joseph asked her to check the door to the cave and the door to the smoke house. She made sure they were closed tightly.

The area at Joseph's homestead was barren that year, until the next spring when the rain came. When the fire started, most of the grasshoppers were either burned up or they moved on.

Rose's thoughts were interrupted. Henry pointed and yelled, "I think it's smoke from the train." They rode as hard as the horses would go. Henry had learned directions from his father at an early age. He was aware the smoke from the train was billowing up but it was coming toward them, instead of going toward the direction of Oklahoma City.

The train was heading back to St. Louis. They both sat and watched as the train moved away from them.

Henry looked at her and said, "Rose, by the time the train arrives back in St. Louis, and then lays over a few days and travels back this far, it will be another week. Do you want to go on, or stop and wait for the train to return?"

"Henry, we need to go on. We could be in Oklahoma City when the train gets back here," Rose said, wondering why she was willing to endure traveling day and night on a horse with Henry.

Henry and Rose traveled as close to the railroad tracks as they could. In some places the tracks were laid after the railroad crew dug through a hill. It was so narrow the horses had no room to walk on the outside of the tracks. They would have to struggle up a steep hill.

Henry would always tell Rose to lean forward on her horse going up the hill. He always led the way, going up one way, then turning, making a large winding circle, so the climb would not be so steep.

Once they were at the top, they started down. Henry told Rose to lay back on her horse, and loosen her hold on the reins. The ride down was dangerous to the rider and to the horse. The hills had trees growing on them. Hitting a tree could be fatal, for it was a fast, straight trip down. Rose always closed her eyes, and put all of her faith in her trusted horse.

While keeping the train tracks in sight, Rose pulled her horse up beside Henry. She mentioned , she had only a few more strips of beef jerky left. Also she asked, "If they could stop at the next settlement and try to send a telegram to her father." Up to now they had stayed away from any settlement or general store in case the man was there or had stopped there.

"I'm sure we can find a settlement if we stay close to the railroad tracks. If the settlement has a rooming house we could get a room. We need to get a meal and clean up," Henry said, knowing how important it was for him to take care of her.

"You will have to sneak me in Henry, no one must see me." Rose told him.

"When we get to a settlement, we'll wait till dark. I'll go in and get a room. Then ask for my meal to be brought to my room. I'll tell them how hungry I am. Maybe they will bring me more food." Henry hoped the plan would work.

"Henry, how do you plan to get me to your room?" Rose asked.

"Rose, I'll do what ever I have to do." Henry replied.

It had been over a week since Rose had slept in her bed at her father's home.

Her bedroom in Joseph's cabin had been small, dark and dirty. The mattress was made of straw. She had taken the mattress outside and beat it to get the dirt and dust out of it. The quilts Rose had taken to the creek and washed each one. They dried after she hung them over the porch railing. The bed frame had spider webs clinging to it. Rose made many trips to the creek for water the first week she was there. Everything in the cabin had to be cleaned.

Rose was riding in front of Henry when she saw some buildings. It was more than a few small stores. This was the biggest settlement they had seen along the way.

They could see movement in this large community. When they were close enough to see a large sign, the name of the town was Springfield.

Children were playing, dogs running down Main Street. The street was filled with horses tied to the hitching posts. Horses, wagons, and buggies were lined up in front of buildings.

People were busy going in and out of the general store. Rose could clearly see fruit on tables out in front of the store. For the first time since starting this trip, she realized how hungry she was. How food had not even been thought of.

The stable was busy. They could see the fire burning as the stable worker mounted metal plates on horses' hooves. They watched as men loaded wagons of lumber from the lumber yard. The swinging doors into the saloon were also busy, swinging back and forth.

Henry pointed to what he thought looked like a rooming house. He told Rose, "I'll go there first and try to get a room."

They remained in the wooded area surrounding the town. They sat on their horses, fascinated by what they could see. Rose had spent the last five years imprisoned at Joseph's cabin. Henry had only left his father's home once in his 25 years before this trip with Rose. They pointed out different things on Main Street to each other that they had not seen before.

The next hour went by, and it was beginning to get dark. The town emptied out. People were leaving in every direction for their homes.

Henry looked around until he found a place he thought Rose would be safe until he could return for her.

Rose sat alone under a tree, wrapped in her blanket, trying to keep hidden. Her horse was tied to a tree a few feet away. The saddle remained on her horse in case she needed to get away in a hurry.

It was like this when the two men came to the cabin searching for her. The men had heard of someone living with Joseph. They came to the cabin to make trouble. Rose remembered how she sat down by the creek, in the dark, holding on to her dog Pal, so he would not bark.

Her only concern was Joseph, alone in the cabin.

It was after Joseph had made the trip into town to see the sheriff about the young men coming on his property that he became ill and died. Rose put her head down and mourned over her old friend. She would never let him down. She would build the hospital and library in his name.

While her mind was miles away, Henry whispered her name. Rose responded with, "I'm here Henry." Jumping to her feet, letting him see how happy she was he was back.

He said, "Rose, I have a room in the back of the rooming house. I can get you in the back door. We must hurry. They're bringing supper to my room. I've also ordered a tub of water to bathe in."

"But what about our horses, Henry?" Rose said, "I'll never part with this horse."

"I'm taking both horses to the livery stable," Henry told her, "I told the worker there, I bought the horse, saddle, and I'm leading the horse home with me."

Henry went first as usual, leading her behind the rooming house.

It was very dark in the alley behind the boarding house, and dogs were barking loudly. Lights were turned on in some of the rooms. Henry hurried her through the back door, and down the hall to his room. The room was dimly lit by one small lamp. The room had one window with a lace see-through curtain. It also had a shade that covered the window. The room had one bed and a nightstand with a wash bowl and a pitcher on top. It had no closet, just some hooks sticking out of a board. In a corner, a tub was filled with water to bathe in. It also had a fold-up screen to conceal the tub.

⧽ Chapter 22 ⧼

Rose sat down on a chair behind the door waiting for Henry. Her hand was holding her revolver that she had taken out of her saddlebag.

Rose looked at the bed and wished she could lay down and sleep forever.

The noise Rose heard was a key in the door, and Henry stepped in. He closed the door, and they heard a knock. Rose stood behind the door while Henry opened it and took a tray of food from the maid. They sat on the bed and shared the food.

Henry leaned over and whispered in her ear, "Rose, you take a bath, I'll lay down on the bed until you finish. Then I'll sleep on the floor."

"Henry, I would not ask you to sleep on the floor. You deserve to sleep in the bed. I trust you completely." She said, feeling better when knowing he would be close.

Behind the screen, the bath was relaxing, and Rose closed her eyes, making her sleepy. The private inlet at Joseph's creek was where she always went to be alone. The vision of the inlet came into her mind. Wild flowers were growing along the bank. Tree limbs leaned out over the water. Someday she would return.

Henry laid on top of the bed. Instantly Rose heard his deep breathing. She finished her bath and put all of her clothes back on.

Because Henry had gone many hours without sleep, waking him took a few minutes. Slowly, he moved behind the screen.

The room was light when Rose awoke. Henry was lying beside her in a deep sleep. Rose looked at this man that had ridden five days and many hours into the night to get her safely this far. She had never known anyone like him.

His eyes slowly opened and he smiled at her.

Footsteps in the hall, just outside of their door was a jolt into reality. Henry sat up and was at the door in a minute, listening. The sound of the footsteps could no longer be heard.

Henry told Rose "Wait 15 minutes before you leave the room. That will give me time to get to the livery stable and saddle the horses. I'll try to send a telegram to your father, too. Pull your hat down on your head and meet me at the place we came into town from. We'll ride around the back part of the town instead of riding down Main Street."

Rose quietly opened the door. The hall was empty. She was behind the boarding house walking close to the buildings, keeping her head down when 2 dogs came up to her. They sniffed her and then started to bark. Rose stopped and talked softly to them. She reached to pet them. They both licked her hand, and their tails were wagging.

One of the dogs reminded her of Pal. Pal was just a puppy when Joseph brought him to the cabin for her. Leaving him behind when she traveled back to St. Louis was very difficult for her. She didn't know how much she missed Pal until now.

The two dogs followed her down the alley and out into the street. She was hoping no one would notice her. But the dogs continued to follow her and jump around her.

Horses and wagons were coming into town. People were on the street now. The stores had their doors open. It was starting to be busy again. The two dogs were making so much noise, people turned and looked at her.

Rose was hurrying along the street when a man yelled, "Hey, boy, come and help me. I can't get this strap on my horse."

Her heart was pounding as she walked to the horse. The stranger pointed to the strap. Rose leaned down under the horse, grabbed the strap, and snapped it to the harness.

He said, "Where you going? You want a ride, jump in the wagon." He took hold of her arm. She pulled her arm away. He grabbed her again. He was dragging her to his wagon. He was getting boisterous, yelling loudly, saying, "You can help me do my chores."

Rose was franticly looking around, and then she heard Henry's voice. "Let's get going." She turned, and Henry was on his horse with the reins of her horse in his hand. Rose ran into the street, took the reins, jumped, grabbing the saddle horn, her foot was in the stirrup, and she was in the saddle. The ordeal left her completely shaken.

Chapter 23

Henry was in a hurry to get her out of town. She rode along side of him. Rose was not going to let him leave her again. The dogs followed them to the edge of town, and then turned around and went back.

Out in the open area, between the trees, the weather was cool. Henry knew they did not have clothes for the winter coming on. He was sure they had a week of long cold days and nights before they would reach Oklahoma City. They kept their horse blankets ready.

The horses had eaten and rested. Henry let loose on the reins. His horse did what he enjoyed doing. He ran at a fast gallop. Rose would never let Henry get away. She stayed with him.

Rose had known nothing about her horse when this unpleasant trip began. But now she felt she knew all about his disposition. He showed his strength and appeared to love competition. After the horses began to breath heavy, they slowed them down to a walk.

They found a wagon wheel track, and traveling was much easier. People had homesteads all around Springfield. Their cabins were made of the trees that had been cleared to cultivate the land. Some cabins had windows, a few had only a door. Creeks were usually close by for water.

The pioneers had corn planted in small spots because of the many trees in Missouri. The fields of corn were being harvested by hand. Families were working together. Each homestead had small children working in the field. Most were dressed in threadbare clothing.

Rose saw women and girls working along side of men and boys. She also knew how hard life could be on the homestead.

She closed her eyes and looked back at the first time she saw Joseph's cabin. It was the opposite of the home she had been raised in. Repairing the cabin enough to live in took her nearly a year.

Joseph's father had built the cabin with the only help from Joseph's mother. Joseph told Rose the story of his birth in the cabin. Most babies were born without a doctor. Women labored for long hours without any medication. If a woman lived close by, she would come to help, when the husband or one of the older children went for help.

Joseph's father had homesteaded so many acres no homestead was near. His father delivered him and cared for him until his mother recovered. His mother had made baby clothes for him out of grain bags and flour sacks. She sewed all of their clothes by hand with a needle and thread.

One of the memories Joseph told her about his mother was the thimble she wore while she sewed. He had given the thimble to Rose.

As a baby, Joseph had been wrapped in a horse blanket for warmth. The only heat in the cabin was from the fireplace. He told her he had been placed in a wooden crate in front of the hearth. Rose never tired of the stories.

Chapter 24

By afternoon, the air felt cold with snowflakes starting to fall. Rose looked up. The clouds looked big and fluffy, and snowflakes were falling out of them.

They each wrapped in their blankets for protection. The horses reached the top of a hill. Henry stopped first and Rose stopped beside him. The view was magnificent.

Rose spoke, "Henry, did you ever see anything so beautiful?" The rolling hills were covered with fresh fallen snow. The evergreen trees turned from green to white, making them look breathtaking. The scenery made the long day's ride less tedious.

Henry agreed with Rose but he knew if the snow continued into the night, it would hamper their traveling. He noticed the rabbits and small animals, like mice, were scurrying to find shelter. The snow was getting heavier.

Henry said, "Rose, I fear if we don't find a place to take shelter, we'll be in trouble. If we find a homestead, we'll ask if we can stay in their barn."

As they encouraged their horses to continue on, the snow was piling up. They looked through the snowflakes, searching mostly in front of them. The dark small building sat in front of a hill. If they had not been looking for cover, they would have ridden around it and up over the hill. As they rode close to it, Henry mentioned to Rose, "The doors look so high."

Henry dismounted, walked to the door and unlatched it. He felt his way through the door. The inside was extremely dark. He took small steps feeling along the wall. The walls he discovered were dirt. His hand felt what he knew to be a lantern. Henry always carried matches in his saddlebag. The lantern gave light to see the room they were in.

Henry explained to Rose what he thought this underground building was for. He said, "This was a barn for the Pony Express riders. New fresh horses were kept here for the riders to change horses. The rider would leave his tired horse here and take a rested horse to continue on."

Rose was aware the building was simply a large hole in the hill. But it was braced with large limbs over their heads. It had stalls for four horses.

Henry closed the large doors to keep out as much cold and snow as they could. Each horse was put in a stall. He gave them some old hay he found in the corner.

Henry began to laugh and said, "Rose, our horses take up the whole stall. The Pony Express horses were smaller with thin legs for running."

Rose agreed and told Henry how much she loved her horse. She went on to say, "I'll never let him go back to that man."

The abandoned barn warmed up from the body heat off of the horses. Henry took the first stall and prepared to go to sleep. Rose was lying in the second stall. Even the noise from the horses eating didn't keep them awake.

Chapter 25

Rose found herself back in Joseph's cabin. To Rose, Joseph was a legend. In Rose's mind his ability and skill to have survived his life in the conditions he lived in was one of the reasons that she admired him so. He was the pioneer that thought of others first. The year all of the crops dried out for his renters, he asked for no rent. Also he bought grain for each renter to feed their animals until the next crop was harvested.

Henry had both of the horses saddled and ready to start another day of traveling when Rose woke. She could hear him talking to his horse, like he did all of the time, as he opened the doors and took his horse outside. He tied him to a tree. He returned for her horse. He cleaned the underground barn to leave it just has they had found it.

Because the ground was covered with snow, and the territory was strange to them, Henry was very precise at the path he directed his horse on. Rose was behind following in his tracks. He led out first at a slow walk.

The look down into a valley below them was a beautiful view. Rose pointed to a herd of deer. They were kicking at the snow looking for food under it.

Wrapped in their blankets with only their eyes showing, Rose felt the peaceful feeling she had felt when she took Joseph on the sleigh rides. She remembered covering him with a warm blanket. She had also put down a warm brick for his feet. The horse had pulled the sleigh smoothly up and down the rolling hills. Joseph loved his land. The thought made her sad. She did not want to dishonor him by not getting the hospital and library built.

The morning went by uneventful. Henry stopped at the edge of a narrow creek. They watered the horses and ate some beef jerky. The horses walked through knee high cold water. They went one at a time up the slope and out of the water. Then entered a new plateau. The land laid out flat. They could see a homestead but it was too early in the day to stop for the night.

Henry stopped and asked Rose, "Can you ride for a few more hours?"

"Of course I can, Henry, I need to get to Oklahoma City as fast as I can," Rose answered.

ᴄᵿ Chapter 26 ᴢᴏ

The snow had melted into the ground making traveling easier. Henry pushed the horses. By late afternoon, Henry found a wagon track going toward a homestead. It was a remote area. There was a cabin and a few small buildings. It looked dark and run down.

Henry walked slowly to the cabin door. He knocked on the dilapidated door. The door opened, and a lady with two small girls looked out at him. The woman was thin. Her eyes looked full of fear. She looked old for being a young mother. She acted timid and was startled to see a stranger at her door. The little children clung to their mother's skirt. The dresses they wore were faded and soiled. They wore no shoes.

From behind her, Henry heard a loud voice say, "What are you doing woman? I want my supper."

The lady told Henry, "I need to tell my husband." She closed the door but Henry could hear.

"A man is at the door." She said to her husband.

The door opened again, and a man looked out at Henry, and said in a demanding voice, "Come in and eat with us."

"No, no thanks. My brother and I just wanted to ask if we can sleep in a shed for the night. Then we'll be on our way in the morning," Henry said.

"No, the man reached out and grabbed Henry's shirt. Get your brother and come in and eat first." The man was not going to give in. The man was close enough that Henry could smell liquor on his breath. The man was definitely drunk.

The man turned to his wife and yelled, "Get the food on the table. We have company for supper. This man and his brother are going to eat with us." He pushed Henry out of the door.

Rose could hear the hollering but not what was being said.

Henry hurried to Rose and told her, "The man has been drinking, and we better do what he says. We'll eat, and I'll do the talking. Rose, you'll have to take your hat off, but keep your head down."

Henry was about to tell Rose how mean and disrespectful the man was to his young wife when the man opened the door. He yelled, "The food is on the table."

Henry and Rose tied the horses to a post. Then walked into the cabin. Two extra places had been set at the table. Rose tried to keep her head down and went right to the table. She could not ask if the lady needed help. The older girl carried the food to the table. Her father criticized her several times about where to set the food on the table. He spoke in a harsh voice to his wife about how slow she was. The young wife said nothing.

Henry sat down and slid his chair close to Rose, so his leg was touching hers. He was always protecting her.

The young wife looked at Rose several times and said, "My name is Mary. My oldest daughter is Elizabeth, and this is Sarah. My husband's name is Jesse Rocker."

The man yelled, "He doesn't care who you are, and he doesn't care about these damn kids either."

Keeping her head down, Rose said, "Yes, I care."

The man was so busy filling his plate, passing food to Henry and trying to eat and talk at the same time. He appeared not to have heard Rose.

The older girl, Elizabeth, looked at Rose, and said, "What's is your name?" Speaking in a softened voice. Rose said, "My name is Joseph, Joseph Higgins. This is my brother, Henry."

The girl's father told her to "Shut up and eat or go to bed." The mother reached over and patted her daughter's arm.

Mary said, "We do not get company. The girls are so happy to see you."

The last few days had been calm and placid for Rose, but suddenly she wanted to pick up the hot gravy and pour it over this man's head. How could he treat his beautiful family this way?

Henry tried to talk to Jesse and keep him from becoming unreasonable, which was not easy.

The young wife had prepared a delicious meal, and Jesse apologized, saying, "It should have been better."

Then he abruptly sent his daughters to bed. The girls didn't want to go but he raised his voice, and they left the table and went up the ladder to the loft that was their bedroom.

Rose wanted to help this young woman. She didn't know how at this time. Especially after the young mother whispered to Henry, "Please take me, and my girls with you."

Henry was as kind as he could be, telling her to wait. He said, "Jesse could hurt you or your girls. I promise I will not forget you, and I promise I'll do what I can for you and your daughters."

Henry and Rose thanked Mary over and over for the food. Henry reluctantly shook hands with Jesse.

Jesse walked to the door, and pointed to the shed they could sleep in. It was a relief to be in the shed where they could talk about what they had just witnessed. They talked late into the night about how they could help the young woman.

The night was not restful. Rose's voice sounded firm when she said, "Henry, I must find a way to help her."

Henry thought to himself Rose was a very kind person but how could someone like Rose; with no home, no money, help someone like this young mother who had two children to care for. Henry had been puzzled at remarks Rose had made at different times about helping people.

 Chapter 27

It was still dark out when they left the homestead. Henry did not want to have to cope with Jesse, and he did not want to see the hurt in Mary's eyes.

Because the land was easy to travel on, in and out of the trees, they made good time. They saw a few more homesteads where the trees had been cleared.

Rose had only known of one other person that had been forced to live in a cabin. The difference, Rose was loved by the man that wanted no one to see her. She was angry when she first came to the cabin. But while being confined, that soon disappeared, and he became her teacher, storyteller, and defender. He lived by the principles his parents taught him.

He was her caregiver; yet she was also a caregiver. He did not allow anyone to see her for the five years she lived in his cabin. Joseph protected her, and then he loved her, knowing the deep-seeded love he felt for her was companionship, gratefulness, and he had always felt indebted to her.

This was not what Mary Rocker had in her life.

Henry thought his horse was getting tired. He was slowing down. Then he realized his horse was limping. Henry pulled his horse up and read a small sign that was nailed on a post. He looked at Rose and smiled. The sign said, "Oklahoma." They were at the border.

The other small piece of wood had an arrow pointing in another direction, and below it said, "Joplin," and below that, said "Carthage, Missouri."

Henry checked his horse and found an open area. It was a tear on the lower part of the leg below the knee. It had dried blood but was still open and bleeding.

Henry told Rose, "We'll have to camp here. I need to clean his leg, and he will have to rest."

Henry looked around for a campsite where they could hide and be safe from any intruders. They needed to start a fire to get warm, but most of all Henry needed light to treat his horse's leg.

Rose helped find firewood and get the fire started. Henry's first priority was to care for his horse. He poured water from his canteen onto his handkerchief to clean the wound. He always carried a small container of salve in his saddlebag.

The cut was deep and caring for it appeared painful for the horse. Rose tried hard to hold the horse from moving. It took several tries for Henry to keep the horse's leg up to clean it and apply the salve. The horse's leg shook with shivers when Henry was done.

Wrapped in their blankets, they tried to sleep. Henry rebuilt the fire during the night. The night was bitter cold. Even having a horse blanket to lie on, and the other one to wrap up in, Rose's body was cold, she pulled her blanket up and covered her face.

Chapter 28

Some of the trees in the area had died. They stood reaching far up into the sky with their dead limbs bare and reaching out like skinny arms and hands. The wind made them move toward their campsite. Rose tried to erase the picture from her mind.

Henry woke early concerned about his horse's leg. He unwrapped the scarf. The leg had a drainage coming from the open area. He again cleaned it, applied more salve and rewrapped it.

Henry explained to Rose, "I'm either going to ride with you, or I'll have to walk until the sore heals over."

Rose answered, "Henry, my horse can carry us both all the way to Oklahoma City. We just can't go as fast."

Henry saddled his horse, brought him up behind Rose's horse. He mounted Rose's horse sitting behind her saddle. The feeling he had was that he wanted to put his arm around her waist to hang onto. Instead he took hold of the back of the saddle with one hand, and with the other he held onto his horse's rein.

As they began a new undertaking, Rose realized she would do anything to help Henry and his horse, and she would do anything to get back to Oklahoma City.

Henry watched his horse to see if he was limping. The horse trailed along with no sign of a limp. Rose was sure her horse could carry them both. He had carried two once before.

Rose saw the water first. It was a stream, and it looked like the shortest way would be to go through it. Henry said, "We'll let the horses drink. Then, on the other side, I'll put fresh salve on my horse's leg."

While riding through the water, they both noticed a small waterfall a short distant up stream. The water rolled over large rocks that were laying in the stream. The country was so beautiful.

They started and soon found they were again close to the railroad tracks heading to Oklahoma City. Rose was sure the land was changing. The land under them looked dry and sandy.

The sky was clear, the sun bright, and it continued to be cold. The wind made it feel much colder. They each had their blanket wrapped around them.

Henry leaned forward and asked Rose, "Can you hear thunder?" Rose responded saying, "Henry, it can't be thunder. Look at the sky."

"What do you think we're hearing? I think I can see some dust coming in our direction. We need to find shelter." Henry's voice sounded serious.

They found a group of trees to stand in and waited to see what was coming. They remained on Rose's horse. Henry pulled his horse up close. He held onto his horse's halter. He slipped his arm around Rose's waist to keep her secure on her horse.

What they saw was a herd of wild horses. It looked as if they were being chased. They were running fast with their heads high. They were running within inches of each other. Their eyes were open with the look of being terrified. Their mane straight back. They were frightened by something.

It was an intense minute before they knew if the horses would come through the trees. Then the first horse turned just as the herd got to the trees, and the rest all followed around the trees. It sounded like a stampede. Even the ground under Rose and Henry vibrated.

A couple more minutes went by, and then Henry and Rose heard what had the horses running to get away from. Six men riding hard, yelling and hollering in loud voices, were in pursuit of them. If the men caught the wild horses, they would belong to them.

Rose was concerned and asked Henry, "How long do you think they will run them?"

"They must have a place where they are chasing them to. A dead-end valley, or they have built a corral to catch them in," he said.

Rose said, "Did you hear how hard they were breathing?"

"Yes but it takes a lot to stop a wild horse." Henry told her.

When they could no longer hear the horses, Rose headed her horse out again with her guardian sitting close.

Chapter 29

The day was long. They made comments to each other about the new land they were traveling in. It was late in the afternoon, and Rose asked Henry if they would camp soon.

Henry replied, "We need to go a few more miles before we stop. We've seen more homesteads, and that means more people are in this area."

Rose had looked at several homesteads and saw the piles of wood piled up next to the cabin. When the fall season came at Joseph's cabin, it meant preparing for a cold winter. Joseph could no longer cut and split wood so his renters supplied him with wood until spring.

Rose was never allowed to open the cabin door after dark. She thought about all of the wood she had carried into the cabin each afternoon, enough to last all night. It had been her responsibility to keep the fireplace burning all through the night. It was after supper each night when Joseph asked her to read to him. Then she fixed the fireplace one more time before she went to her room.

The sun was going down when Henry said, "Let's stop. I need to check the soil. We're in a wet area. Your horse's hooves are sinking into the sand."

The trees ahead looked dead with so many broken-off branches twisted, sticking up from the wet ground. They looked gray and white, as if they had been like that for a very long time. The trees were in a murky region, where water had been standing and now had dried up to sand and mud.

Henry slipped off of Rose's horse and turned his horse around to lead him out of this devastation. This would take more time. They would have to backtrack to dry ground, then make camp and start out when it was light in the morning.

Henry unfolded the map his father had drawn for him. His father had traveled this territory as a Pony Express rider a long time ago.

Henry and Rose studied the map and found they were near a lake lying to the south of them. A short distant to the north was a river called Neosno River. Henry explained to Rose, "This is the edge of a lake called Lake of Cherokees. We need to go north.

They made the usual preparations of camping for the night. Henry made some coffee and Rose unwrapped some beef jerky. She also mentioned to Henry how low their supplies were getting. After eating they rolled up in their blankets and were soon asleep.

Henry woke Rose and hurried to get started for another long day. This would be the first day that he would ride his own horse since his horse had torn open its leg.

The bright light from the sun helped them pick their way through the damp ground and fallen trees. This was going to be their most difficult day of traveling.

For a short distance the horses were moving freely. Then their hooves began to sink. Henry had chosen what he thought would get them past this swampy country. The horses were trying hard picking each foot out of the dark, thick mud. Henry held his arm up and turned his horse slowly in a more northerly direction. He needed to get the horses on dry land before one stepped on a rotten limb under the mud and perhaps break a leg.

It took most of the morning to get back to where they had started. Henry told Rose, "We need to let the horses eat, drink, and rest at least a couple of hours before we start again."

ᴄᴣ Chapter 30 ᴤᴄ

Henry checked the map again. This time they would go even further north. The map looked like they would have to cross the Neosho River.

"We cannot let the river stop us, Henry. Please Henry, we must get across" Rose said as she bowed her head and wept. Henry walked to her and reached for her hands and arms and placed them around his neck. She looked at Henry with her eyes filled with tears. He leaned toward her, tilted his head, and did what he had thought about doing for a very long time.

Rose responded to his kiss not knowing why. She was feeling afraid and insecure. And yet she did not push Henry away. She kissed him back. Rose stood with her body pressed up against his, needing to erase all of the restraints in her life. Needing to find contentment, instead of always feeling the fear of failing.

The situation that had brought them together was now changing into another, perhaps complicated relationship.

Henry whispered in her ear, "Rose please, forgive me. I didn't mean to complicate your life even more. My feelings for you are sincere. You are a wonderful woman. Any man would be fortunate to have you."

"Henry, you have done so much for me. How can I ever repay you?" Rose asked trying to find words to help them both through this predicament. She could not pursue any relationship with Henry because of John Fitzpatrick whom Henry did not know about. However, she did not regret kissing Henry. She was attracted to him.

"Rose, you do not owe me anything. I'm happy to spend this time with you and for you. I'll get you to Oklahoma City. I promise," Henry said, feeling somewhat guilty for what he had done.

The horses had rested nearly two hours when they turned them north. They would have to cross the river in its deepest part. Henry guided his horse along the bank of the river. Rose followed closely behind him. He was looking for an easy way to enter the river.

Henry stopped his horse and told her, "Be careful and stay in the saddle. Hold on to the saddle horn. Rose, if you get off of the horse, make sure you don't get kicked by your horse's hooves. Please, Rose, if for any reason you get off, stay next to your saddle."

The horses stepped slowly off of the shore and into the deep water. The drop-off was sudden. Only the horse's heads were showing. They were holding their heads up as high as they could.

Henry yelled while in front of Rose, "Rose, hang on."

The water was moving swiftly. Both horses were swimming rigorously. Rose could hear her horse breathing hard as he pushed toward the other side of the river. Henry was doing well Rose thought.

Then Rose's horse put his head down, and jerked it up hard out of the water. Rose was not expecting this and found she was not holding on well enough. She was pitched into the water. Her horse was swimming as fast as he could. By the time she came back up to the surface, he was far out in front of her.

Henry turned his head around to make sure Rose was right behind him. A shock of disbelief shook his body. A look of horror appeared on his face. He tried to turn his horse around. The current was so strong. It took Henry a few minutes to make the horse understand they were going back.

Rose was an excellent swimmer but now she was fighting hard. She was pulled under by an under current. She fought, kicking desperately to come up. Her clothes were heavy, and her work boots made her feet feel immovable. Her head came out of the water, and she gasped for a breath of air. Then she went under again.

Henry was yelling, "Rose, Rose, I'm coming, hang on."

He had seen her go under, and he was sick to his stomach. He wanted to jump into the water where he had seen her go under. If he did, he knew they would both drown because he was not a good swimmer. Henry thought if he could throw her his rope, he could drag her to shore.

He tried to get close to her, but not close enough for his horse to kick her. Henry screamed, "I'm throwing the lariat, Rose. Grab it, and I'll pull you to shore."

Rose was going down the river fast. Henry's horse was getting tired. He threw his lariat. Rose went under, then reappeared. She came up near where the lariat had landed. But Rose was unable to catch it.

Henry jabbed his legs hard into his horse's sides. He needed his horse to get closer when he threw the lariat again.

A hand came up out of the water first, then Rose was out enough to grab the rope. She was holding on as tight as she could.

Henry headed his horse to shore to pull Rose out of the water. She turned over on her back and lifted her head up every so often to get air. The minute she was on dry ground she let go of the rope.

Rose laid just on the edge of the water, coughing, trying to get the water out of her lungs. Henry leaped off of his horse and ran to her. While she lay on her side, he patted her back firmly.

She was choking up water until she collapsed from exhaustion, and she was shaking from being extremely cold.

Henry gathered wood and started a huge bonfire. He wrapped the two horse blankets around her and told her to remove her overalls, shirt and soaked boots. He hung her clothes and boots next to the hot fire. He also sat her as close as he could to the heat.

Henry was concerned Rose would think he was hardhearted for not wanting to jump into the water. He did not want her to think he was afraid either.

When Rose warmed and was clear minded, she asked about her horse. Henry told her he had seen her horse make it to shore.

He said, "We'll have to go back along the river. I hope he stopped when he got out of the water.

Rose, I could not have saved you if I had jumped in the water. You see, I cannot swim well."

"Henry, I'm so grateful to you. You saved my life. You risked your own life. I'm sorry." Rose said with tenderness in her voice.

Henry thanked her for her kindness. He then said, "While your clothes are drying, I need to ride back and look for your horse."

The area was about a half mile back along the river. He found the hoof prints coming out of the river. He followed a couple of miles but did not see him. Henry decided to go back and get Rose, come back, and follow the tracks.

Chapter 31

When Henry arrived back to Rose, she was up and dressed in her dry clothes. She wanted to go after her horse. Now, it was her turn to ride behind Henry on his horse.

The fire was completely out when they left to track her horse. Henry took her back to show her the tracks coming out of the river.

They followed the tracks. The tracks went into and out of a wooded area. Then they started into a rocky area where they lost the tracks.

They traveled until late in the day. Rose was beginning to feel she had lost her beautiful horse. She thought back at the many miles they had traveled together. The horse had been so energetic, strong, and always high spirited.

Henry refused to travel on the rocks and boulders when it was dark. They camped early and talked about starting again in the early morning light.

Rose wrapped up in her blanket and tried not to think about someone else finding her horse. And even worse, if someone else found him and claimed him as their own.

Rose wanted to delay the start of a new day. This could be the day she had to admit she would never see her giant, steadfast, dauntless steed.

Henry and his horse were ready long before Rose. The day was cold, and they each wrapped the blanket around their shoulders as the hunt for Rose's horse began. Rose reminded Henry again about how low their supplies were getting.

Henry was aware how risky it was for his horse walking on the large rocks. If he made an error stepping or slipping one foot off of a cutting rock. If he would stumble, he could break one of his legs. Then they both would have to walk the rest of the way to Oklahoma City.

Henry was worrying with each step his horse took. They were close to an edge. He suggested it would be safer if they walked and he would lead his horse through this rugged area.

Rose walked ahead and tried to find Henry and his horse a less dangerous trail.

The opening was a surprise. The rocks and boulders stopped. They walked on small stones and gravel, and then the bareness stopped. They could see some ground with soil. A spear of grass appeared. It was eaten by Henry's horse as they walked by it. Looking ahead, they could see more grass.

The horse's pace picked up, and Henry was running toward the grass. The horse was eating, devouring the grass as he walked.

Rose caught up and sat down on a grassy spot to rest. She watched Henry's horse move and eat. She thought about her horse, and she hoped who ever had him would be kind to him.

Henry's horse had turned away from her, and she heard him whinny. Then he whinnied over and over. Henry and Rose looked at each other puzzling. Rose jumped to her feet and listened.

She heard what she thought was an echo. Rose stared in the direction she thought the whinny was coming from.

What Rose saw coming as fast as he could was the horse she thought she had lost forever. He stopped and bucked, kicking his back feet in the air.

He was coming back to her. He trotted right up to her. The saddle was intact. The reins were dragging along on each side of his head.

He had some scratches, a few small cuts. Henry applied salve on each one. But he acted like he did before he was separated from Rose. She mounted him with gladness in her heart. With the reins in her hands, she again felt she would make it back to Oklahoma City.

Chapter 32

Early the next morning, it started to rain. They hurried, getting ready for the strenuous day they would have. Henry had used the last of the coffee. The beef jerky was gone, too. He knew they had to stop at the next settlement for supplies. His objective each day was always to make as many miles as the horses could. Henry was impatient to start. Finding a settlement would take time.

Riding in the cold rain made them wrap their blankets over their heads. The rain started lightly, and then became a hard rain. The horses moved slowly. Henry decided if the rain continued for a long time, they would have to find shelter until the rain stopped. Once their blankets were wet, it would be miserable to travel.

The ground was becoming soggy. The horses were walking in mud. Rose was shivering from the cold, wet blanket. Henry pulled his horse over for Rose to ride up beside him.

Henry told her, "The first town, we'll have to stop. Even if it means going out of our way in a different direction."

They were out in an open area with no trees to get under. They both rode hunched over in their saddles. Henry's horse wanted to stop but Henry kept encouraging him to keep moving.

Chapter 33

Rose yelled at Henry when she thought she had seen a light. It was not straight ahead, it was off the trail that they were on. As they got closer, they could see two lamps burning in a large room. The street was full of mud. The wagon wheel tracks had water standing in them.

There were no horses tied to the railing in front of the building. Beside the building was a roof held up with poles. Several horses stood tied up out of the rain.

Henry rode his horse under the roof, and Rose followed. It was a relief just to get out of the cold rain. They tied their horses to the wall, wiped the horses off with their wet blankets.

Henry walked toward the room with the lamp. Rose walked close behind him. The room was a saloon. One lamp sat on the bar, lighting up the men standing at the bar drinking. The second lamp sat on a table where some men were eating. The room had two tables. One table was empty, it was near a pot bellied stove in the middle of the room.

The stove was full of burning wood. Giving off warmth, life-saving warmth for them. The stove was black in color and was big around. It had a black stove pipe going up to the ceiling. It was about as hot as it could get without blowing up. A small amount of smoke smell filled the room.

Rose took a chair next to the stove to dry her clothes. She also was trying to hide. Henry went up to the bar and asked the elderly, heavy set lady, "Madam, could my brother and I get some food to eat?"

One man at the bar said, with a nasty sound in his voice, "You got money to pay for food, you no-good saddle bum?" Henry did not look at him, nor did he answer him.

"Of course, young man, you can eat all you want. I'll fill two plates," she said. Henry thought the woman looked like she had worked hard all of her life. The lines on her face had dirt in them, but her eyes looked kind. Her hair was disheveled; the dress and apron she was wearing had food stains down the front. The black marks on her apron looked like ashes from the stove. She had to empty the ashes, and filling the stove, Henry guessed, was also her job.

"Hey man, you sure got a sweet-looking brother," one man at the bar said.

"Too bad he's not a girl," another man said.

The first man said, "Why don't we sit at your table with you and your little brother?"

The woman said, "No, you guys stay right where you are. These two are going to eat by themselves." She added sternly, "You leave them alone."

"We just want to get to know them." The first man said after taking another drink.

Henry knew he could not let Rose be alone. These men sounded like they had been here drinking most of the day because of the rain.

The woman brought a plate of food for each of them. She leaned down and whispered, "When the rain stops, you fellows be on your way. These men can be dangerous. I've seen them when they get boozed up and mean. I'll pack food for your saddle bags."

The men at the bar began to bicker. Their voices were getting louder. The lady behind the bar reached for her gun.

She yelled, "Stop, or get out and go home."

"You won't use that," one man said.

The woman held the gun up and screamed back, "I will use this on you if you don't behave."

The men quieted down and mumbled to each other. One said, "Let's have some fun." They put their heads together and made a plan.

The lady returned to Henry's table, she had a large bag full of food, for their saddlebags. Henry paid her, and they both thanked her.

"I would advise you to get going as these men are planning something," she said, warning them. "When you go out of the door, I'll lock it and stand in front of it with my gun. You must hurry."

Henry stood up, carrying the bag. He turned to Rose, and said, "Stay close to me. When you get to your horse, get your gun from your saddlebag. Get on your horse, and we'll get away if we can before someone gets hurt."

Rose carried the blankets that had dried by the potbellied stove. Henry took big steps, and Rose trotted beside him with her hand on his coat tail.

She jumped upon her horse, reached into her saddlebag for her revolver while backing her horse out from under the cover. Henry was at her side as they entered the street.

The three men were stumbling out of the bar door. They tried to run to their horses. They were about two minutes behind Henry and Rose.

Henry headed out with the certainty he had to protect Rose, and he would do anything. If he had not had Rose to protect, the three men would have had the fight of their lives. They would not have survived Henry's wrath.

Rose was right beside Henry. She was trying so hard to keep Henry from getting hurt. They rode side by side with horses that somehow felt the urgency to run from danger.

Chapter 34

The three men were trying to catch them. They also had the advantage for they knew the area. Henry and Rose did not.

Ahead of Henry, he could see something at the side of the road. It was crosses sticking up from what he was sure was a cemetery. He steered his horse to the cemetery. Rose was beside him.

Henry yelled, "Rose, get off of your horse. Hide in the cemetery. I'll return for you." He grabbed her reins and headed back on the trail to lead the three men away from Rose.

Rose laid down in the dark, wrapping her body around the bottom of a cross. Her worry was not about herself. But her worry was about Henry. What had she done to his life?

So many people had touched her life in the last five years, such good people. Joseph Higgins, John Fitzpatrick, and now

Henry and all of his family. The young woman and her daughters whom they ate with in her cabin and stayed the night in a shed on her homestead. The woman in the saloon, who fed them and helped them to escape. Rose wondered if the three men hurt her pushing her away from the locked door.

Rose would not forget the kind people she had met on this long journey.

Horses were coming. She could hear them coming fast. Rose never moved. Then they were slowing down.

"Rose, Rose," Henry had come back for her. He was safe. She hurried to the outline of the horses.

"We must hurry, Rose. When those men wake up from their tumble off of their horses, I think they're going to be mad. I'll tell you what I did this evening."

The ride was fast and in a different direction. Henry hoped they were going toward Oklahoma City. He did not have time to stop and look at the map. Henry had been reliable, taking charge, and doing what he thought was best for her. Rose continued to ride willingly as she had done so far. They rode until the morning dawn.

Chapter 35

What they did not know was they were riding on sacred ground. Before they realized where they were or what was happening, Henry and Rose were surrounded by angry Indians.

The Indians brought their horses up close, so no one could move. They were talking and their voices sounded agitated. This ground was holy to them.

Henry reached over and took Rose's hand as if to say, I'm sorry.

Then the leader turned his horse, and everyone followed him. With Indians in front and in back and all around. They were being escorted from the sacred ground and into the Indian village.

Rose had only read about the teepees Indians lived in. Henry had learned about Indians from his mother's home-schooling.

The valley was covered with large and small teepees. Small bonfires were burning close to each tent. The camp was quiet at first, then it erupted, and it was like a beehive. Children, women, and young men were running along side of Henry and Rose.

They were taken into a tent. The elder Indian leader sat next to a young woman and her small child. Rose sat down next to Henry, and they all looked at each other. They looked at each face.

The young woman smiled at Rose, and said, "Do you remember Jo Jo?"

Rose took a deep breath, smiled, and said, "Oh, yes, I remember."

Rose remembered everything about the birth of Jo Jo. The mother had given birth to her son in a grassy area along the creek that Rose did Joseph Higgins' wash in. The same creek Rose had swam in for the five years she had lived with Joseph.

Seeing the young mother and her son again, made Rose more determined than ever to return to Oklahoma City. The hospital she planned to build would let anyone in who needed care. It did not matter to Rose whether their skin was light or dark. No one would be turned away.

The young mother told Rose the story, why she and her husband had been at Joseph's creek when her baby was born. They were coming from her husband's homeland, and they thought they could make it home before the baby arrived.

"At that time, I was not allowed to talk to a white person." She went on to say, "Thank you, you were so kind, gentle, and I understood everything you said to me. When you talked about Joseph Higgins with such respect. You said, he was such a peaceful man. I chose my son's name because of you."

Henry and Rose spent the night in a teepee. They were offered a drink. It was tea made from wintergreen. They were handed a piece of meat that had been smoked over an open fire. Henry guessed it was buffalo.

Buffalo skins laying on the floor were what they were sitting on. The Indians covered up with buffalo hides at night for warmth. Hides hung all around the inside of the teepee to keep the cold out.

Henry and Rose drank and ate with their gracious hosts. Knowing this could have turned out very different if Rose had not helped deliver the chief's grandson.

They rested, wrapped in buffalo skin.

When the sun came up the following morning, the young Indian mother rode with Henry and Rose to the edge of the Oologah Reservation and then pointed them toward Oklahoma.

They were both silent at the beginning of the morning ride. Rose had so much to think about. The young woman gave them each a buffalo skin to wrap in as they rode in the cold morning.

The small boy had not known Rose, but he knew Rose was special to his mother. He gave Rose a silver bracelet. It had the letters CHEROKEE engraved on it. The Indian tribe was proud of their heritage.

By late that morning, they were in an area where they came upon wagon wheel tracks. Rose pulled up beside Henry where they could talk to each other.

Rose told him, "You showed me how brilliant you are. You communicated with the chief, even though you could not speak his language. If we had tried to escape, we could have been hurt. You are truly an honorable man."

Henry studied her face and wondered to himself if he could ever win her heart. He noticed she wanted to stand closer to him, and in the tent she sat close enough to him, that when her legs were crossed, her legs touched his. When she touched him, he always felt the same little tingle surge through his body.

Rose did not know Henry was listening to her every word when she told the Indian woman about him.

Rose had told her why she was traveling with a man she was not married to. She had told her he was a lot like Joseph Higgins, kind and extraordinary. He was a wonderful friend. He lived his life like his mother had trained him as a child.

Henry wanted more than friendship with Rose. But he also knew Rose was strong, and a man could not force her to do what was not to her liking.

Rose said something that bewildered Henry and he did not know how to answer her. She said, "Henry, would you help me build a new hospital and library?"

He answered slowly, trying not to hurt her feelings. "Rose, I would do anything for you but Rose, it takes money to build a building."

"I know Henry, I know," She said. When the time was right she would tell him, she was one of the richest women in Oklahoma. Right now she had no proof.

It would be a little hard to prove this to him now. Riding on a horse she took form the man. She was dressed in boy's clothes and wearing a pair of boy's boots that did not belong to her. Her hair was cut short and was all lengths. Her fingernails were broken off, her hands were full of scratches, and most of all, she had no money on her.

Henry's family had given him most of their savings to get Rose to Oklahoma City. And now it was almost gone, and they still had many miles to travel.

Rose was aware of the money Henry had spent on the boarding house, food and care for their horses in the stable. She wondered how long it had taken Henry's family to save it. She hoped to repay every cent and more.

Chapter 36

The wagon tracks had more paths leading away to homesteads. Rose noticed some roofs were made of wood, and some had thatched roofs made of straw, or thick layers of wild grass. She also noticed some homes were completely covered, or made of the wild grass, mixed with mud.

The roof Joseph had on his cabin had been damaged from age, wind, and extreme weather changes and drying out from the sun. The first year Rose was there, the cover of snow would melt, and along with rain leaked into the cabin. The heat from the fireplace rose and warmed the inside of the roof, making the snow melt. It took her a long time to get all of the roof recovered.

The crop of corn in the area they were passing through had been picked and stored for the winter. Some farmers had no place to store the corn so it laid in several piles on the ground. If a farmer had cows, they were grazing in the corn stocks. Rose welcomed the sight as they had ridden through some desolate areas.

They met several riders, buggies and wagons. Rose kept her head down and always looked away. They had cowboys ride by, hooting and hollering. Rose wondered if they had been visiting a saloon somewhere.

The route they had chosen was becoming busier. Children walked along the road, coming from school. They each carried a lunch pail. The pails were silver, and all looked alike. Rose recognized them as being pails lard came in. Some carried their books in bags made from feed sacks. The children all wore shoes but Rose was sure they would take them off when they got home to save them for good.

Chapter 37

While they rode, Henry was studying the map. He located the lake that they were approaching. They sat on their horses in awe of what they were watching. It was close to winter, and thousands of geese were migrating and had stopped on the lake to rest. Some had landed, and others were flying in. The geese were large; their wing span was over three feet in length. The birds sat down on the water with their huge wings extended.

Their colors were magnificent. Their brilliant colors of white, black, and some had a necklace of red on their long, powerful necks. The sound coming from the lake was an uproar of vigorous, high spirited, excessive quacking, and honking. The big birds would rest overnight and resume their flight at dawn.

Henry pointed to a sign on a tree stump with the words Tulsa, Oklahoma, printed on it. Some letters were not visible, but he had seen it on his father's map. He was sure now they were heading in the right direction.

It would take at least two and one-half more days to get there. And they had eaten all of their food so Henry needed to stop while it was still light to hunt. He could have shot one of the migrating geese but the shot would have rang out, and the geese would have killed themselves in a desperate flight.

He motioned for Rose to ride beside him. He told her they needed to camp, and they would have to hunt meat for supper. They rode, wanting to find a small spot hidden from view. Henry turned his horse off of the trail and continued riding. Off in a low valley, Henry saw some old buildings. They stopped and watched for awhile to see if someone was living there. Then they slowly rode to the homestead.

Weeds and brush had grown over the path to the cabin. Henry motioned for Rose to tie her horse to a post. He said, "I don't think anyone has lived here for a very long time. I'll go in first and check the cabin."

Henry walked slowly up to the door. The door opened easily as he stepped inside. No one was living here. It looked as if it had been abandoned years ago. Rose entered the abandoned cabin with uncertainty. Henry found a lamp setting on a wooden table in the middle of the room. The lamp had only a small amount of kerosene in it. After a few minutes, Rose could see how much the cabin looked exactly like Joseph's cabin.

She pictured in her mind Joseph sitting in his rocking chair in front of the fireplace. One morning as he sat intently watching her prepare his breakfast for him, he suddenly confessed his love for her. But he was a gentleman, knowing his love for her was only an honorable emotional feeling.

Henry interrupted her thoughts, by saying, "I'm going out. You need to get your gun from your saddlebag. Then, stay very quiet and do not go to the door. If I'm not back, stay here until morning, then go on alone."

Rose answered with a low firm voice, "Henry, I'm going to wait right here until you return."

Rose sat in the rocking chair with her loaded revolver on her lap. She put her head back, and it felt so peaceful to be here. Why did this family leave everything behind and what were they so afraid of that they took nothing with them?

She would never leave here without Henry.

Rose wondered why the family that had worked so hard to clear the land and build this home left it. A doll made from cloth was lying on the floor. A gun carved from wood lay beside it. If only she could have helped them.

Hunting was something Henry did well. He had provided food for his large family many times. It was dark when Henry returned but he had shot and cleaned two rabbits.

Rose started the fireplace, and the rabbits were placed on a rod over the fire. After they had eaten, the remaining meat would be taken along for the next couple of days meal.

Henry mentioned the farmer left all of his belongings, even the horse's harnesses were hanging in the barn. He went on to say, "I think something bad happened here."

"Henry, do you mean someone died here?" Rose's voice sounded as if she needed an answer now.

Henry answered her, trying not to frighten her, "I don't know for sure, Rose, but I found an axe lying in the yard in front of the barn. It had a crust on it. I think we need to rest a few hours then leave before morning. I don't want to get caught here."

⊂ Chapter 38 ⊃

Rose sat in the rocking chair trying to relax and sleep. Henry was asleep within minutes. Rose could hear his heavy breathing. She decided someone should stay awake and guard the cabin.

Henry had been asleep nearly two hours when Rose heard what she thought was a horse whinnying. She slipped out of the rocking chair and crawled across the floor to Henry. She gently put her hand on his arm, and he woke instantly.

Rose whispered, "I heard something outside."

"Rose, hurry. We need to get to the back door now. Do you have your gun?"

When Rose answered, "Yes," she was on her way to the back door. What she heard coming through the front door made her body tremble.

"It's him." She instantly recognized the language as Spanish. The one person she feared most, spoke in his native tongue most of the time, and that was in Spanish.

Henry and Rose were out the back door when Henry whispered, "The horses are tied behind the barn." Without hesitation, they hurried toward the barn.

The horse Rose had heard was the intruder's horse.

The dark cold morning made Rose shiver, she slipped her arms through the buffalo arm holes, and she was ready to ride. Her horse was moving as always, with vigorous power.

They left the homestead, and after a distance, Henry stopped his horse. He turned to Rose and said, "You start out, and stay off of the main trail."

"No, Henry, no. You come with me. The man is dangerous. He will kill you to get to me. I'm not going to let him do that." She was trying to warn him enough so he understood they needed help from the law.

"Please Henry. We'll go to the next settlement and tell the authorities." Rose had never been so fearful after seeing that man again.

Henry could see on her face if he did not go with her, she would do something they would both regret later.

Henry pulled on his horse's rein without answering her and headed back on the trail leading to Tulsa. Both horses were eager to start. The ride would be hard for over two days, depending on how long the horses could keep up a fast pace.

Rose rode with the fear that the man could catch them. At times, she laid her head down on her horse's mane and just hung on.

The railroad tracks were heading into Tulsa. Henry was staying as close as he could. He felt it would get them to the sheriff sooner. They did not stop to rest until late in the afternoon when they found a small stream off of the trail.

Henry and Rose ate small pieces of the leftover rabbit. Rose had had no sleep the night before, and she was weary. The worry she had was that the man would hurt Henry. And she could not and would not let that wicked man hurt a brave, strong but gentle person like Henry.

Rose rode her horse up along side of Henry and said, "I'm so afraid if the man sees his horse, he'll make trouble for us."

"No, Rose. He'll have to kill me first." Henry said forcefully.

"Henry, this man has been relentless. He has dogged me for two months. Nothing will stop him. He wants me as his own, and I will go with him to protect you."

As Henry looked back down the trail behind them where they had just came from. Henry saw some riders coming fast. He reached over and took hold of one of Rose's reins, he pulled her horse to follow his horse off of the trail and into a wooded area. He made sure they were not seen from the trail.

Chapter 39

He then asked Rose to watch for the riders as they passed. She sat feeling cold and alone. The four riders were in a fast gallop. Rose had no doubt whom she had just seen.

Henry did not have to be told. He saw Rose's body become limp, telling him the man was looking for her, and he was very close to finding her.

Henry said, "We need to go deeper into the trees. We'll stay here tonight. We have one more big day before we make it to Tulsa."

"Rose," he continued slowly, "if they have a telegraph office, we can contact your father in Oklahoma City. I have just enough money to buy you a ticket to ride the train the rest of the way."

Rose sat on her horse quietly listening. If she got on the train in Tulsa, she knew she would never see Henry again. That was not what she expected or wanted.

They rode until they found a campsite they both felt safe in. Henry gathered wood to build a small fire. The leftover rabbit would be shared, and then their food would be gone again. Henry had a few grounds of coffee left. They each had one cup of coffee.

Rose laid down on her horse blanket. Henry's warm body lay next to her. They covered up with their buffalo skins. They looked up into a sky that was filled with beautiful stars. The noises they heard were the horses stomping their feet and an owl hooting. After Rose heard the cry of a pack of wolves, she told Henry about the night at Joseph's cabin when she was surrounded and attacked by one.

Henry reassured her. His gun was lying beside his hand.

Lying beside Henry, suddenly she realized she had not thought of John Fitzpatrick for a very long time. She had thought of her father each day. But John had not been on her mind recently like he had been before she began this pilgrimage.

The warmth from her buffalo cover and the long day of riding were enough to put her to sleep immediately.

Chapter 40

When Rose awoke in the morning, the sun was shining on her face between the large giant trees. Rose opened her eyes, and Henry was gazing down at her. He smiled, and said, "Good morning, Rose. Your horse is ready and waiting."

Rose returned his friendly greeting. She asked for a few minutes of privacy like she had done each morning. She went into the trees. Rose needed to prepare to start the long day's ride. She was in a squatting position, and by the time she heard the rustle of leaves and dried grass, a creature unexpectedly stood within a few feet of her.

The long snout and vicious sharp teeth hanging down out of each side of its mouth made her freeze in fright. His eyes looked huge. They were big and brown. And her position was eye to eye contact.

His hair was rough and straggly. His skin was dry, dirty, and crusty. She noticed a few bird feathers stuck to his mouth as if he had just found and devoured a dead bird.

Rose slowly, cautiously struggled to pull up her overalls as she rose to stand upright. The animal took a step closer as Rose took a step backward. She quickly made the decision not to run.

The large tree next to her was a safe place to step behind. The animal moved to the tree and started around it. Rose quickly stepped to the next tree, and she could hear the animal moving faster.

He was making a heinous grunting sound of anger. She moved on to another tree. She stopped to listen for his movement. Rose could hear his feet stepping down on the brush lying on the ground. She could hear that he was nearly running. He seemed to know where she was and what tree she was hiding behind.

Rose's Triumphant Return

Rose finally figured out he was following her scent. He could smell the horse smell she had on her clothes. Then she remembered the buffalo hide she covered up with while she rode and covered up with at night.

The animal kept coming, and Rose continued to step deeper into the trees. She stood behind a tree and then another. At this point, she decided the animal was not going to give up.

All of the trees were looking the same to Rose. She had been so busy trying to lose the animal, when suddenly she came to the realization she had wondered far enough into the trees, that she was lost.

She didn't know what direction she had come from because she had stepped behind trees in different directions.

Rose was sure this animal could not climb a tree so the next tree with a limb hanging down, she grabbed the limb. She pulled herself straight up. The next limb was close enough for her to reach so she pulled herself up and stood on it.

Rose stood on the limb and watched as the animal found her again. He had his snout down on the ground and was smelling her odor. He came up to the tree and lifted his head in the air. He made a penetrating harsh grunt at her. He circled the tree several times, and then abruptly laid down next to the tree.

Rose was standing on one limb and hanging on to one above her head. The noise she heard was hard to hear but the limb she was standing on felt like it had moved downward. The next time she heard the cracking sound, she was looking for another limb to move to.

Rose was struggling to step upward. She had one foot upon a larger branch when the limb she had been standing on fell to the ground. She quickly pulled her other foot up. The falling limb disturbed the animal. He jumped to his feet, made a disgusting sound, and finally wondered off into the trees.

Getting down, Rose knew would be harder. The main branch was now gone. She moved around the tree holding on firmly. She lowered herself to the limb under her. Then she again heard a noise of crushing of leaves and branches moving. Her first thought, the animal was coming back.

Chapter 41

Then she heard Henry's voice, he was calling out to her.

Rose yelled as loud as she could, "I'm here Henry, I'm here."

Henry hollered one more time as he was getting closer. She answered in a clear loud voice. As soon as Rose saw Henry from the top of the tree, she yelled, "Up here."

In disbelief Henry looked up, and Rose looked down seeing the look on his face. At first it was a slight smile, then he broke into a boisterous laugh. This was the first time Rose had heard him laugh. She thought he had a wonderful laugh but she wished he would have picked a different time.

He waited patiently while she climbed down the tree. When Rose mounted her horse, she vowed she would always take her revolver with her, wherever she went.

She would tell him later why she was up in the tree. After all, he did laugh at her.

The long day's ride started to Tulsa. After they were back on the trail, they both wrapped up in their buffalo skin. Rose pulled her hat firmly down over her head.

At first, it was only a cool mist in the air. Then, as the time passed, it began to rain. Before long, large snow flakes appeared. The snow flakes covered the trail. They continued to move slowly.

Traveling in the darkness, while it was snowing was very dangerous. No lights, or warning of horses, wagons, and buggies could be seen. Henry was listening intently.

Henry was trying to get to Tulsa, Oklahoma, as soon as he could. He needed to get food for them both. Suddenly, Henry heard a wagon coming. He stopped and grabbed Rose's reins, pulling their horses off of the trail.

Horses pulling a wagon were hurrying into Tulsa. Several miles ahead, they could see lights coming from windows, shining into the street.

They rode into town and Henry was looking and searching for a stable for their horses. They rode down Main Street. It was late at night, and the town was still busy at the saloons and boarding houses.

Henry located a stable and found it had one stall vacant. The man in charge put both horses in one stall. Henry removed the saddles and rubbed both horses down. He paid the man in charge and now they had just enough money to buy some food to eat, and also to send a telegram to Rose's father in Oklahoma City. They had no money to be able to sleep in a room in a boarding house.

Henry asked the man in the stable if he and his brother could sleep in a corner of the tack room. The man hesitated and said, "Two other men want to sleep there, too."

Henry answered with a positive statement, "That's O.K. we'll manage with them." He glanced over at Rose, she nodded her head at him knowing Henry would protect her.

Chapter 42

They hurried to the closest boarding house. There were only a few people left eating. Henry picked a table close to the door and away from anyone else in the room. The last time they had eaten was the night before when they had eaten the last of the rabbit.

The cook came to the table and told them he had just enough food left for them. Rose looked at his shirt, and it was a colored feed sack. The color was faded from being washed. The other things on his shirt were food smears from early in the morning, until this hour late at night. Rose closed her eyes and thought only of the food she wanted.

Henry asked the cook about sending a telegram to Oklahoma City. The cook told Henry the telegraph office was located in the stage coach office, and it opened early in the morning.

Henry paid for their food, and they left, heading for the livery stable. They slipped in quietly. Henry stepped in first. Rose stood very close, directly behind him. He walked her to their horses.

Then he whispered to her, "Slip between our horses to the manger. Crawl into the manger and pull any hay that's left over you. I'll be very close."

Henry squeezed between the horses in the next stall, and crawled into the manger. He whispered, "Rose, I'm right next to you."

Knowing Henry was close to her, she went to sleep with no fear.

Rose woke when Henry was putting the saddle on her horse. She crawled out of the manger, and backed her horse out of the livery stable. Henry led the way to the telegraph office.

Henry could not leave the horses on Main Street. If the man was near and saw his missing horse, he would take the horse away from Rose. Henry decided the best place to hide the horses would be out of town.

They rode looking and watching. Then they found a homestead with children out playing. Henry asked if he could tie their horses to a tree by the yard. The older boy agreed it would be alright for the morning.

Henry led the way to the telegraph office. He took Rose in the office with him. He thought she would be safer in the office.

Rose noticed the two doors. One said women, and the other said men. This was the first time she had ever seen an indoor outhouse. She looked at Henry, and he realized she needed to go in one. The man in the office cage was looking out at them.

Henry lowered his voice in a whisper and said, "Go in the men's, and I'll stand outside the door."

"Henry," she said, "What if someone is in there now?" He stepped to the door, knocked and entered, leaving her for only seconds.

The outside door opened and without stopping to ask, the dark skinned man went into the men's room as Henry was coming out. Henry looked directly at the man, and then as he walked to Rose, she had turned to face him.

All Henry said was, "Rose, that's him."

Rose answered softly, "Yes."

Henry moved Rose up to the window, beside him, and sent the telegram. The way Rose had instructed him to. The telegram was addressed to John Fitzpatrick at the bank in Oklahoma City.

"John, I am in Tulsa, Stop, Please come, Stop. Bring money. Stop. Meet me at the sheriff's office. Stop. Rose.

They were leaving the office as the man stepped out of the men's room. Rose was in front of Henry, and had her hat pulled down low almost over her face.

Henry took large steps, making Rose run along side of him. He walked through the alleys to get out of town. He looked straight ahead. He wanted to get to their horses. They would hide out somewhere until John came to Tulsa.

Chapter 43

The land was flat so they could see the town stretched out for many miles. They needed to find a deserted spot. It took awhile before they found a small stream for the horses to drink and they could wash up in.

When evening came, Henry told Rose they would ride into town, and he would walk her into the sheriff's office. Then he would hide the horses.

The story Rose told the sheriff took them late into the night.

Rose heard the train whistle first. She hoped to see John step down from the train. Henry, the sheriff, and Rose watched as each passenger stepped down.

John Fitzpatrick stepped off of the train. He looked exactly like he did the first time she had seen him when he met her getting off the train in Oklahoma City five years ago.

She said, "John, I'm so glad you are here." He was looking at her but she was not dressed like she had been when he saw her last, when she had gotten on the train to go to St. Louis to see her father.

John said, "Rose, is it really you? Why are you dressed like that? Where are your nice clothes? What happened to your beautiful hair?"

This was not what she had wanted him to say.

"John, I have a long story to tell you. But first, I want you to meet the sheriff. Then I want you to meet Henry. He is the man who saved my life and has traveled with me from St. Louis by horseback. He has cared for me and protected me with his own life in danger. We have been together for over a month."

The two men stood only a few feet apart looking into each other's eyes.

John Fitzpatrick was not going to just give her up to Henry without a fight. And Henry's character was gallant but always prepared with the skill of being confident in what he wanted. He knew who he wanted. He refused to be intimidated.

Rose slowly walked between the two men. She could feel the tension. This was not over.

Henry turned his attention to Rose, "What did you want to tell me Rose?"

Rose was concerned about how Henry would react to hearing she was very wealthy. Henry had been born to a young couple in Missouri. His grandfather had staked the land out and lived on the homestead until his life ended. Henry's father loved the home. He brought his new bride to the home where they started their family.

Life was very hard for a large family. Henry's life had known only giving and sacrificing for his many sisters, brothers and the cousins who came to live with them after his aunt had died.

Henry had traveled with Rose for nearly a month protecting her. Always putting her first. When he was told by his father to ride with her to Oklahoma City, he had mixed feelings. He had never been away from home, never been responsible for keeping an angry, hostile man away from a beautiful young woman that he did not know. But in the month he had been with her, he had fallen deeply in love with her.

Henry stood with his hands in his pockets clinking together two pennies. It was all the money he had left from his father and mother's savings. But he had brought her safely to Tulsa.

The sheriff was going to help capture the man who had kidnapped her off of the train.

Henry felt a stabbing feeling in his heart, because now, what does he do? His obligation to Rose was over. She would be reunited with her father in Oklahoma City.

Henry was feeling he was no longer needed in Rose's life.

Her voice was soft and she hoped she could say it so it would not change the friendship they had between them.

"Henry," Rose whispered, "I'm going to my room to clean up, and then we'll talk."

John walked out of the room with Rose. He slipped his arm around her waist but no one saw Rose's body stiffen.

Henry felt he had just lost her to John Fitzpatrick.

Henry turned toward the door and went out onto the street. He needed to check his horse, and he needed fresh air. He had no money to get a room, or money to buy new clothes.

He decided to get his horse and start home. This trip would be different. He could sleep anywhere, and take time to hunt for his food. He gave the livery stable worker his last two pennies and apologized for not being able to give him more.

Henry saddled his horse, feeling sad and defeated. Most of all, he was missing Rose Donlin.

He started out of town. He would have no problem finding his way home. He rode down Main Street, not seeing the beautiful young woman looking out of the window of the boarding house with her eyes filled with tears.

Rose ran out of her room and down a flight of steps. She ran out onto the street. Henry was no where to be seen. She ran in the direction he had been riding.

A voice behind her was calling her name. She stopped, turned around and saw John was running toward her. His voice sounded alarmed, "Rose, you cannot be out on the street until the sheriff arrests the man that kidnapped you. Please, Rose, you are safe now, Let me take care of you."

Rose tried to hide her tears.

Henry had reached the edge of town, riding hunched over his horse. He was wrapped in his buffalo hide. His horse would take him home while his thoughts were on Rose.

He yearned to smell the pines and just be alone with his broken heart. He hoped the next month of riding would help erase her face from his mind.

Rose entered her room and mentioned to John, "I need to be alone for a while." John knew better than to question her.

Rose could not let Henry disappear out of her life. She had to make a plan. But she needed to go on to Oklahoma City to take care of her father first.

Later, she left her room wearing the clothes John had ordered and sent to her room. The dress was covered with black lace. The long sleeves had lace hanging over her hands. The full skirt was black and white stripes made of taffeta with black lace over it, too.

She had boots laced up over her ankles. The coat was exactly like the one she was wearing on the train when the intruder kidnapped her. But somehow, Rose was not happy over all of her wealth when she pictured Henry, riding alone, with no money to buy food on his journey home.

John wanted to get her out of Tulsa as fast as he could. He also wanted to get Rose away from Henry. He bought two tickets to ride the train back to Oklahoma City.

Rose watched as her horse was loaded in a cattle railroad car. He walked up the plank as if he knew this was what Rose wanted him to do.

John sat as close to her as he could on the train. He tried to talk to her. He told her he had her satchel at the bank. He had retrieved it out of the closet on the train.

Rose laid her head back and closed her eyes. Henry was laughing. She was standing on a limb up in a tree. That was the first and last time she had heard him laugh.

She just wanted to look at him and see his beautiful face, know his kindness, and feel his strength. Rose had watched him each night when he removed his hat. His curly hair would tumble down on his forehead.

Rose had not heard him complain once on their long trip. He never raised his voice. His calmness always kept each situation tolerable and under control. He always helped her saddle her horse and start the campfire. He always gave her time to get ready for their ride each morning. He was a very patient man.

Rose remembered Joseph telling her once, "When a man treats his horse and dog like a friend, he is a good man." Henry treated his horse like a friend. She was so grateful to him, and she did not get to thank him before he left.

The train felt as if it was traveling at a high speed, and it was taking her further away from Henry.

When John and Rose stepped off of the train, the walk to the bank took them only a short time. John gave her the satchel she had hidden from her captor. She asked him if he would check her horse and take him to one of her renters' homesteads.

Rose met her father at the boarding house. He cried with her and whispered, "Rose, I'm so glad you are here. I thought something terrible had happened to you."

"No father, I'm fine. I'll tell you about my trip later." She said with sadness in her voice. "First, I have to find an eye doctor for you."

Rose moved into a room next to her father in the boarding house. She opened her satchel in the privacy of her room. Everything was in order. The deed to her land needed to be put in a safe at the bank. She counted the money that Joseph had kept in a box under his bed. It was a large amount. Her plan for the money was to send it to Henry and his family.

Rose emptied the satchel, wrapped the money in the towel that was in her room, and laid it back in the satchel. She needed to find a way to get the satchel to Henry. She had no idea of his address or where he and his family lived. It was dark when she had found their barn in a rain storm. Then, when she left Henry's home, it was late at night.

Rose knew she had traveled for three days after the man had forced her off of the train. The train had traveled from St. Louis only a short period of time. She thought the train depot would have a map of the tracks they traveled on. She needed to look at it. She also knew the man could be on the street.

Slipping out of her room, walking as fast as she could, she stopped at a general store and bought a black hat with a black veil. It covered her hair and face completely.

The young man working in the depot was anxious to help Rose. He told her all of the stops the train made on the way to St. Louis. Rose studied the map and tried to point out where Henry lived. She remembered they watered their horses in a stream on the land his family owned. The land had small areas of cleared land along with areas of many trees. She could not pinpoint the exact area.

Her next decision was to send a telegram to where she thought the nearest settlement was. She sent the telegram to the law enforcement office. In the telegram she asked if the Helgens family lived in their vicinity.

Rose explained to the young man she would return the following day to see if she received an answer.

The walk back to the boarding house was lonely. Her mind would not stop thinking about Henry Helgens. She missed him by her side.

Rose would not let him go.